MOON CHILD

/ / / /

J.R. RAIN

THE VAMPIRE FOR HIRE SERIES

Moon Dance
Vampire Moon
American Vampire
Moon Child
Christmas Moon
Vampire Dawn
Vampire Games
Moon Island
Moon River
Vampire Sun
Moon Dragon
Moon Shadow
Vampire Fire
Midnight Moon
Moon Angel

Published by
Crop Circle Books
212 Third Crater, Moon

Printed in the United States of America.

ISBN-13: 978-1546858294
ISBN-10: 1546858296

Dedication
To Sandra...thank you for always being there!

Acknowledgments
A big thank you to Sandy Johnston, Eve Paludan and Elaine Babich. My crew.

"To be immortal is commonplace; except for man,
all creatures are immortal, for they are ignorant of
death; what is divine, terrible, incomprehensible, is
to know that one is immortal."
—Jorge Luis Borges

"The only thing wrong with immortality is that it
tends to go on forever."
—Herb Caen

"They entertain us: they dance for us, sing for us,
play for us. But most important, they bleed for us."
—*Diary of the Undead*

1.

The ocean swept beneath me.

The waxing moon reflected off the rippling
currents, keeping pace with my swiftly racing body.
White caps appeared and disappeared and once I
caught the spraying plume of a grey whale
surfacing.

Some mothers would fault me for leaving my
son's side, I knew this. Some would even fault me
for saving the life of a little girl while my son is sick
in the hospital, that I should be by my son's side at

all times, no matter what. I get it. No doubt some would feel that I should be beating down doors looking for a cure, not resting until my son is healthy again. I get that, too.

Below me, a seagull raced just above the surface, briefly keeping pace with me, until I pulled away. I dropped my right wing, angling to starboard. The beaches appeared, and soon the exorbitantly expensive homes. A party was raging in the back of one of them. I passed in front of the moon, and I spied one or two of the party-goers looking up, pointing.

But I'm not like most mothers. In fact, I would even hazard to guess there are very few of us, indeed. I could *see* my son's imminent death. I could *see* the doctors failing. I could *see* it, feel it, *hear* it.

And not only that, I knew the hour of his death, and it was approaching.

Fast.

The beachfront homes gave way to marshy lands which gave way to beautiful condos and hillside homes. I swept over UCI and into a low-lying cloud which scattered before me, dispersed by my powerfully beating wings.

I had a decision to make. I had the biggest decision of my life to make. So I had to think. I had to get away, even for just a few minutes to sort through it. I had to know that what I was about to do, *or not do*, was the right decision.

Until I realized there was only one answer.

I was a mother first. Always first, and if I had a chance to save my son, you better damn well believe I was going to save him.

I flapped harder, powering through the cloud and out into the open air. My innate sense of navigation kicked in and I was locked on to St. Jude's Hospital in Orange.

2.

It was late when I swept into the parking lot.

I circled just above the glow of halogen lighting, making sure the parking lot was indeed empty, before dropping down next to my minivan.

To think that this hulking, winged creature owned a five-year-old minivan with license plates that were about to expire was laughable. No, it was incomprehensible.

I wasn't worried about security cameras. They would capture nothing...except maybe a car door opening and closing...followed later by a spunky, thirty-seven year old mother who may or may not fully appear in the image, depending on whether I wore make-up. Without make-up, the camera would capture only the curvy outline of empty clothing.

Of course, knowing that I did not appear on camera prompted me to remember to wear make-up, including a light coating on my arms and backs of my hands. Still, no doubt there were hundreds of surveillance videos out there of an unseen woman. Want to know how to find vampires? Check surveillance video.

For now, though, I alighted near the van's cargo door, which itself faced a listless magnolia tree. The tree was surrounded by some low bushes and curved pipes that I assumed had something to do with the hospital's plumbing. But what the hell did I know?

The area wasn't quite big enough to accommodate a hulking, mythical monster, and I ended up trampling some of the bushes, breaking a branch and denting one of the pipes.

Life goes on.

In my mind's eye, I saw the woman in the flame, watching me calmly, waiting. I focused on her, and she seemed to move toward me, or I to her. I was never sure which. The feeling that came next was difficult to describe, since there really was no feeling. As if awakening from a short nap, I gasped lightly, and raised my head. I was on one knee, which was digging into a small spider plant that had seen better days. I fluffed up the little plant and stood. Next, I reached under my fender and found the small hide-a-key that I kept there.

Shh. Don't tell anyone.

I unlocked the minivan and slipped inside. My

clothing was still there, and a few minutes later, after a quick dusting of foundation, I emerged from the minivan, purse in hand. The transformation from giant monster bat into a concerned mommy was now complete.

My life is weird.

I checked the time on my cell. It was just after 2:00 a.m. I would say the *vampire's hour*, but the truth is, any time between sundown to sunup are the *vampire's hours*.

My daughter Tammy was staying with my sister, and no doubt they had all gone home by now. After all, Anthony appeared, to all those concerned, to be fairly stable. It was only me and my heightened extrasensory perception that suspected that not all was as it seemed.

Indeed, I knew my son had only hours to live. If that.

I had taken some of that time to come to a decision.

And I had made my decision.

With the waxing moon overhead shining its silent strength, a strength I seemed to somehow draw from, I turned and headed for the hospital, knowing the staff there would allow me in to be with my sick son.

A sick son, I thought determinedly, *who would be sick no more.*

3.

"Hello, Samantha," said Rob, the front desk security guard. Rob was a big guy who probably took steroids. You know there's trouble when the night shift at a children's hospital knows you by name.

I said "hi" and he smiled at me kindly and let me through.

At the far end of the center hallway was a bank of elevators. As I headed toward it, I heard a vacuum running down a side hallway. I glanced casually at the cleaning crew working away...and saw something else.

Crackling, staticy balls of light hovered around the cleaning crew. Many such balls of light. I knew what these were now. They were spirits in their purest forms. Some called them orbs, and sometimes they showed up on photographs. Many non-believers assumed such orbs were dust on the lens. But the camera could never fully capture what I could see. To my eyes, the balls of light were alive with energy, endlessly forming and reforming, gathering smaller particles of energy around them like mini-black holes in outer space. But there was nothing black about these. Indeed, they were often whitish or golden, and sometimes they appeared red. And sometimes they were more than balls. Much more. Sometimes they were fully formed humans.

As I swept past the hallway, a cleaning lady looked up at me. I smiled and turned my head just as one of the whitish electrified balls seemed to orient on me. Soon it was behind me, keeping pace with me.

I just hate being followed by ghosts.

And as the elevator doors closed in front of me and I selected the third-floor button, the ball of white light slipped through the elevator's seam and joined me for a ride up.

It hovered just in front of me, spitting fire like a mini sun. It moved to the right and then to the left, and then it hovered about a foot in front of my face.

The elevator slowly rose one floor.

"It's not polite to stare," I said.

The ball of light flared briefly, clearly agitated. It then shot over to the far corner of the elevator and stayed there for the rest of the ride up.

The doors dinged open and I stepped out onto my son's floor.

Alone.

***

Danny was there, sleeping.

He was sitting in one of the wooden chairs at the foot of the bed. His head had flopped back and he was snoring loudly up at the heavens. Probably irritating the hell out of God. One thing I didn't miss from living with the man was all his damn snoring.

Well, that and the cheating.

My son wasn't snoring. He was sleeping lightly. A black cloud hung over him, a black cloud that only I, and perhaps others like me, could see.

And it wasn't so much as hovering as surrounding him completely, wrapping around his small frame entirely. A blanket, perhaps. A thick, evil blanket that seemed intent on obliterating the bright light that was my son.

The lights were off, although I could see clearly enough. The energy that fills the spaces between the spaces gives off an effervescent light. These were individual filaments, no bigger than a spark. By themselves, the light didn't amount to much. But taken as a whole, and the night was illuminated nicely.

For me, at least, and others like me.

The frenetic streaks of energy often concentrated around the living, and they now buzzed around my ex-husband, flitting about him like living things, adding to his own brilliant aura, which was presently a soft red with streaks of blue. I have come to know that streaks of blue indicated a state of deep sleep. The red was worry or strong concern. So, even in sleep, he was worried.

Worried for our boy.

Danny was a bastard, of that there was no doubt. He had proven to be particularly nasty and sleazy and underhanded. He was also confused and weak, and neither of those qualities were what I needed in a man. I needed a rock. I needed strength. I needed confidence and sympathy.

Not all relationships are meant to last forever, I had read once. And forever is a very long time for a vampire.

I stepped through the room and over to Danny's side. His snoring paused briefly and he shivered inexorably, as if a cold wind had drifted over him.

Or a cold soon-to-be ex-wife.

I touched his shoulder and he shivered again, and I saw the fine hair along his neck stand on end. Was he reacting to my coldness or to super-naturalism? I didn't know, but probably both. Probably some psychic part of him was aware that a predator had just sidled up next to him. Maybe this psychic alarm system was even now doing its best to awaken him, to warn him that here be monsters.

But Danny kept on snoring, although goose bumps now cropped up along his forearm.

I shook him gently and his snore turned into a sharp snort and I briefly worried that he would swallow his tongue. Then next he did what any woman would want to see.

His eyes opened, focused on me, and he screamed bloody murder.

And he kept on screaming even as he leaped backward falling over his chair, which clattered loudly to the floor. He landed on his back with an *umph*, as air burst from his lungs. He kept on trying to scream, but only a wheezing rasp came from his empty lungs. He scuttled backwards like a clawed thing at the bottom of the ocean.

I stood there staring down at him, shaking my head sadly, knowing that he had attracted nurses from here to Nantucket.

"Are you quite done?" I said, standing over him and shaking my head at the pathetic excuse for a man.

He clutched his chest and stared at me briefly, and then he seemed to remember where he was. But he was still having trouble breathing, and that was scaring him, too.

"Just calm down," I said, kneeling next to him and taking his hand. "Calm down, you big oaf, and relax. I'm not going to eat you. Yet."

I patted his hand as he continued clutching his chest. And then his lungs kicked into gear and he took a deep breath, sucking in half the oxygen in the room.

"Sorry," he said weakly, as running footsteps

sounded in the hallway. "You scared me."

"Ya think?"

I stood and pulled him up with me. Perhaps a little too roughly. He flew up to his feet and seemed surprised as hell to find himself standing.

He looked around, mouth open. "Jesus, Sam. You never cease to amaze me."

Just then a nurse rounded the doorway, hitting the lights. She looked first at Anthony in his bed, and then at us. She saw the toppled chair and our proximity.

"It's okay," I said. "I just startled Danny."

"I was sleeping," he said, lamely. He shot me a glance. "You know, nightmares."

The nurse studied us some more, then came over to Anthony's side and checked him out. Satisfied, she left, although she looked back one more time as she exited.

Danny studied me for a moment or two and seemed like he wanted to say something. His hair was mussed and there might have been a welt developing on the side of his head. Whatever he wanted to say, I really didn't want to hear it. Instead, I looked over at Anthony, who had stirred a little during the commotion. He almost appeared to be watching us, except his eyes were still closed.

"How is he?" I asked.

"The same, I think. He woke up about an hour ago and asked where he was. I told him he was still in the hospital and that he would be going home soon." Danny looked away. "And...he shook his

head and said he was sorry and that he loved me."
Danny fought to control himself. "I asked him what
he was sorry about...and he said for...being a bad
boy and for...leaving us. He said he has to go but
that everything will be okay."

"He said that?"

Danny covered his face and nodded, words
briefly escaping him. After a few deep breaths, he
tried again. "Jesus, Sam, what the hell is he talking
about?"

"He was probably just dreaming."

"But he was *awake*. He was looking *right at me*.
And he didn't look sick, either. He
looked...peaceful. Good God, he was even *smiling*."

"Calm down, Danny—"

"But what's happening, Sam? Is he dying? Does
he know that he's going to die or something?"

"Don't talk like that."

Now Danny was shaking. Violently. He was
going into shock, or something close to shock. No
doubt a thousand different emotions and chemicals
had been released into his blood-stream. I reached
for his shaking hands and this time he only slightly
recoiled.

"I can't lose him, Sam. I can't. I don't know
what I'll do without him. He's my baby boy. My
little partner. He's everything to me, Sam.
Everything. I'll quit my job to spend more time with
him. I'll do anything to have him back. Anything.
Jesus, we can't lose him."

His words continued on, but they had turned

hysterical and incomprehensible. Before I realized what I was doing, I pulled the big oaf into me and hugged him tight.

But I did not share his tears. Not this time.

Unlike him, I knew there was hope.

When Danny had cried himself out, holding onto me a bit longer than I was comfortable, I showed him to the door and told him to go home and get some rest and that everything was going to be okay.

He paused only briefly at the doorway, checked his pockets automatically for his cell, wallet and keys, then nodded once and slipped out of the doorway, wiping his eyes.

I briefly watched him go, then I turned back to my sick son.

Who would be sick no more.

4.

I stood by his side.

Opposite his bed, rain began pattering against the hospital window, lightly at first and then stronger.

Something wants my attention, I thought.

I ignored the rain, even as a strong gust of wind now shook the window, which was hidden behind the closed blinds. I ignored the rain and the wind and reached down and stroked my son's hair. My narrow fingers slipped through his hot tangled locks. He was too hot. He was too sick. He wasn't going to make it. I knew it all the way to the very depths of my being. His vitals hadn't registered anything yet, but they would.

Soon.

I continued stroking his hair. He seemed to be getting hotter by the second. He also shifted toward my touch, moving toward me imperceptibly, making a small, mewing sound.

The rain picked up, drumming now on the window.

My heart was racing, and for me that's saying something. I continued standing by his side, knowing that this was my one chance to turn away. To not do this thing. I had been advised that he had fulfilled his life's mission, and that it was time for him to move on. I had been advised by a very powerful entity that my son was meant to die. That it had been ordained so, or some such bullshit.

Well, fuck that.

I was his mother. I carried him in me for nine months, I stayed up with him countless nights, bathed him, fed him and worried about him daily. I loved him so much that it hurt. I loved him so much that I would kill for him. I loved him so much that...

I would give my life, my soul, my eternity for him.

I was his mother, and I was ordaining— declaring, dammit—that he would live. And lord help anyone who tried to stop me.

I knew I could be damning him forever. I knew this, understood this, but I also knew there was a glimmer of hope. The medallion. Reputed to reverse vampirism. I had always figured I would seek its answers for myself.

But not anymore.

Now I would seek its answers for him. At all costs. I would devote my life to finding a way to turn him mortal again, to give him back his normal life.

And in the meantime, how would I explain to him what I had done to him? I didn't know, but I would think of something.

Later.

For now, though, time was wasting. My son was growing dangerously hot. I reached down and touched his narrow shoulder.

"Anthony," I whispered, leaning down, speaking directly into his ear. "Wake up, baby. Mommy's here...and everything's going to be okay."

5.

It took a few more tries to awaken him, but I finally succeeded.

He emerged slowly from wherever he'd been. I suspected that place was the blackest of depths. Then again, perhaps not. Perhaps he'd been in heaven. Perhaps he'd been playing on streets paved with gold. Or, more likely, playing Xbox with Jesus.

Only to return here, with me, sick as hell in a hospital and ready to die. Perhaps had I let him be, he wouldn't have suffered. Perhaps he would have slipped out of this world and into the next with ease and little pain.

Perhaps.

He awakened slowly. As he did, a part of me

screamed to let him sleep. If a nurse came in now, she would have been furious.

What am I doing?

"Mommy?" He squirmed under my arm.

"Hi, baby."

"What's happening, Mommy?"

I'm saving your life, I thought. *I'm saving it the only way I know how.*

"How would you like to feel a little better, baby?" I whispered, and it was all I could do to keep my voice steady, to keep it from cracking with fear and uncertainty.

Anthony turned his sweating face toward me; his eyes focused on me for the first time. As they did so, I was surprised by their strength and ferocity. Despite the darkness, he seemed to look deeply into me.

It was hard to imagine that this strong-looking boy was dying, but the black halo hadn't retreated; indeed, it was thicker than ever, and I saw his impending death as surely as I was seeing him now.

"They're waiting for me, Mommy."

I started shaking my head. "No, don't say that."

"It's okay, Mommy. I'll always be with you. Forever and ever."

"No, baby, please don't say that."

"I'm supposed to go soon, Mommy. They're waiting for me."

I was still shaking my head, crying, whimpering, rocking, holding him tightly. Too tightly. "Stop talking like that, baby. We're going to get you better. I have some medicine for you."

His eyes narrowed, studying me in the darkness. He then turned his head and looked to the right. I looked, too, and saw something I wasn't prepared to see. The light energy near the window seemed somehow brighter, more frenetic, more alive. Something was there, something had materialized, but I couldn't see what. At least, not clearly. Whatever it was, it wasn't a human spirit, that much I knew. It was somehow brighter and it radiated a warmth that I could feel from across the room.

"He wants me to tell you something, Mommy."

I was crying now. I couldn't stop my emotions. I wanted to be strong for my son, but I couldn't. I just couldn't. This was too much for me.

"Who, honey?"

"The man in the light."

I tried to speak but I couldn't. Sobs burst from my throat. Finally, I said, "What...what does he want to say?"

But I knew what he was going to say, didn't I? That my son was only here on earth for a brief time. That he was meant to pass on at a young age, a death that was meant to help others grow. That he was here to fulfill some cosmic karma bullshit. I didn't want to hear it. What mother wanted to hear that?

My son was quiet for a moment, cocking his head slightly, listening. Then he smiled broadly. "He says that he loves you, Mommy. That he has loved you from the beginning of time, and will always love you. Forever and ever." He paused, smiling at me serenely, and now I saw now a golden light around his face. The light shone through even the blanketing darkness. My son looked beautiful, angelic. He cocked his head again, and listened some more. "He wants me to be strong for you." My son's face turned somber, and now he was nodding...a very sad and solemn nod. "He says you are making the best choice you can. He wants you not to be so hard on yourself."

"I don't," I gasped, my words strangled, "I don't understand what's happening."

My son reached out, took my hand. I could barely see him through the blur of tears. He said, "Mommy, sometimes it's okay not to understand."

The words came from my little boy, but they were not his own. They were from someone older and wiser, and I felt again that I was speaking directly to his soul.

"But I don't want to lose you, baby. I can't bear the thought. I couldn't live. I wouldn't know how to live. But I can help you. I know how to help you. You can stay here with me. Is that what you want, honey?"

He squeezed my hand, and now he stroked my hair gently, his little fingers running through my matted locks before they gently turned my face toward him. "Of course, Mommy."

I sensed that he was making a great sacrifice. I sensed that he was postponing heaven to be here with me now.

"He's telling me there are many paths a life can take, Mommy. There are many alternate routes to the main road—" Hearing my little boy say *alternate* was just surreal— "We are going to head down an alternate route, a longer route. But we'll still get there, Mommy, eventually."

My son paused, looking over at the warm source of light. He squeezed my hand.

"He's going now, Mommy. He wants you to know there are no wrong choices. Do what you have to do to be happy."

Now the light near the window began to fade, and as it did so, my son turned somber. A moment later, his eyes shut tightly.

"Anthony!" I cried, suddenly terrified. But he was still breathing. Barely.

"Mommy?" His voice sounded weak, tiny. It wasn't the same voice I had just heard.

What the hell was going on?

"It's me, honey," I said, sounding weak myself.

"I feel sick, Mommy." He was hotter than ever.

"I know, baby," I said, as I pushed up the sleeve of my sweatshirt. "I know, and I have some medicine for you."

I brought my exposed wrist to my mouth, paused briefly, and then bit down.

6.

The hospital was nearly silent. The hum of machines. Light murmurings. Beeping somewhere. Actually, lots of beeping.

But now another sound filled the air. This one had been barely distinguishable at first, but now it was growing louder. And not just louder. More frequent, too.

It was the sound of drinking, slurping, swallowing.

At first, I had let the blood from my wrist drip freely into his mouth, although a lot of it didn't actually make it into his mouth. Some of it had spilled down his chin, and I had acted quickly with tissues from his bedside table to catch the stray droplets before they stained his sheets and gown, and led to unwanted questions.

But as more blood passed through his mostly closed lips, he began to react. First, his tongue appeared, swiping at the blood. Then his lips parted.

And then he swallowed.

He made a noise then, a strangled gasping noise, and as he did so, I saw something remarkable. A soft white light issued from his mouth, briefly hovered before the bed, and then faded away.

And just as it faded away, my son reached up and gripped my wrist with surprising strength, and held onto it tightly as he drank from my wound.

And he drank and drank.

My blood. My tainted blood. I'm horrible. I'm a horrible mother. I'm a ghoul. I should be locked away. But you're saving him, dammit. You're giving him a chance to fight another day.

I was a wreck. My mind was a wreck. My heart was a wreck.

As my son suckled from my wrist—reminding me briefly of the babe who had suckled at my breast so long ago—something else amazing happened, something that made me realize there was no turning back.

The black halo began to recede...to be slowly replaced by a faint silver shimmering, emanating perhaps an inch or two from his body. My son's beautiful natural golden and red aura was nowhere to be seen.

It's happening, I thought.

And still my son drank from my wrist. I could

feel the blood being drawn from my arm, sucked into his ravenous mouth. The instructions had been quite clear: You will know he's had enough when you begin to feel weak, as weak as you do in the presence of the sun. The instructions had come from a fellow creature of the night. A much older creature of the night. It was, she said, a fine balance of giving him enough but also not depleting myself.

In the hallway, I heard footsteps. In fact, two sets of footsteps.

They're coming.

And still my son drank, biting down onto my wrist hungrily, drinking great gulps of blood from my open wound.

The footsteps were just outside the doorway. I could hear urgent talking now.

The weakness hit me with a shudder. I gasped and yanked my arm away, tearing some of the flesh. My son's drinking had kept the wound open, kept it from healing supernaturally, as it was inclined to do.

But now as I pulled it free, I could already feel it closing, healing. I grabbed tissue from the bedside table next to me, and had just wiped my son's lips and chin when the lights flicked on.

Doctors and nurses rushed in, and as I stepped aside, I discreetly wiped the blood from my wrist and pocketed the crimson-stained tissues.

***

The cause for the alarm had been simple enough.

My son's heartbeat had rapidly decreased, so much so that the heart monitors had alerted the nursing staff.

I stood back, watching the nurses and doctors swarm over my son, and as they swarmed over him, my son sat motionless. Fully alert and awake.

Watching me.

7.

While the doctors fussed with my son, I stepped out of the room and headed quickly for the elevators.

My hands shook the entire way down, even when I held them tightly together. As I stepped past the receptionist and security guards, I found myself cursing God, the Universe and everything in-between for putting me in such a shitty situation. The security guard said something to me, but I couldn't hear him. I hid my face and walked quickly out into the night. Certainly, this hadn't been the first time he'd seen an upset mother.

Outside, I took in a lot of air, filling my dead lungs, walking in tight circles, running my hands through my hair. I was a wreck. The tears flowed.

What had I done? What had I done to my baby boy?

You saved him, I thought. *You saved him, dammit.*

I fished out my cell phone from my handbag and called my rock, the man I had leaned on for so long, the man who had been just a name until recently. Now he was a name and a face...and teeth.

"It's late, Moon Dance," he said, his voice groggy. He yawned loudly, smacking his lips a little. It was only recently that my relationship with Fang had graduated from instant messaging to phone conversations and even personal meetings. Even so, I was still getting used to the gentle sound of Fang's voice. A mellow tenor, so different than Kingsley's deep baritone. "How's your son?" he asked.

I told him much better. Much, much better, and he snapped awake instantly. I filled him in on my night, a night that had taken me from the depths of the Pacific Ocean, to my son's side, and feeding him from my bleeding wrist.

Fang said nothing at first. As he digested this information, I realized that just by hearing his soothing voice I had calmed down enough to stop my hands from shaking. As I waited for Fang to speak, I saw a man standing in a nearby pool of light, smoking and looking up towards the heavens. The gleam of tears on his cheeks was evident. A children's hospital in the dead of night is not a good place for a parent to be.

Finally, Fang said, "So, you really did it?"

"I had to."

"I'm not judging, Moon Dance. Actually, I think you made the right choice. A brave choice."

"Then why do I feel so horrible?"

"Because it's the unknown. Because it just happened. You saved your son, honey. He's alive because of you. Because of his mommy."

But I couldn't escape the feeling of being selfish, that I had exposed my son to something dark and horrible just to keep him alive, just to keep me from dealing with a lifetime of heartbreak.

"You're not being selfish, Sam," said Fang, using my real name, which he rarely did. He also read my thoughts, which was of no surprise since he and I had developed an unusual psychic connection over the years. And meeting him recently for the first time had only enhanced that connection. "It's your job to look out for your son. It's your job to keep him safe from harm."

"But look what I've done to him."

"Only temporarily, Sam. Remember the medallion."

"But what if it doesn't work?"

"But what if it does?" he countered.

"You're ever the optimist."

"My friend is a gloomy vampire. Someone has to be the optimist in this relationship."

"But what about the psychological harm? I mean, even if I can turn him back, will he ever have a normal life again?"

The man smoking nearby snubbed out his cigarette. He glanced at me once and I saw the darkness around his heart. I didn't know what that meant, but I suspected its implication: someone close to him was going to die. I tried to smile and he tried to smile, but in the end, we only stared at each other with empty eyes as he slipped back into the hospital.

Fang was thinking hard on his end. He was always thinking hard for me. Always helping. Always working through my problems with me.

"It's because I'm a helluva guy," he said, picking up on my thoughts.

"And because you're obsessed with vampires."

"Well, someone has to be. Now, speaking of vampires...six years ago, after your attack, when did you first realize that you were something, ah, something different?"

"When did I first realize that I was a vampire?"

"Yes."

"Weeks later. But I knew something was vastly wrong only a few days later."

"But did you suspect you were a vampire?"

"No. Not at first. I just knew something was wrong."

"When did you crave blood?"

"A few days later."

"How many days later?"

I thought back to my time in the hospital, and then to my first few days at home. "Four days. But I thought I was low on iron or something."

I had an image of my son drinking blood and it was almost too much to bear. I started pacing again and hating myself all over again.

"Calm down, Moon Dance," said Fang, despite the fact that I hadn't said anything, so pure was our mental connection. "The way I see it, you have four days to find him a cure."

I stopped pacing; he was right.

He went on. "You have four days before your son realizes that something is wrong, that he's something different."

"Four days," I said. Relief flooded me. My God, he was right. I had four days to find a cure.

"Four days, Sam, to unlock the secret to the medallion."

"I gotta go," I said. "Love ya."

The words caught him by surprise, as they did me.

"Love ya, too," he said after a short pause, and clicked off.

8.

I checked on my son.

According to the doctor on staff—a young guy who could not have looked more bewildered—Anthony's fever was dropping at an astonishing rate, even though the fever hadn't appeared to break; as in, my son hadn't yet broken out in a sweat.

More astonishing, at least to the doctors, were his eyes. Red, swollen eyes were a hallmark of Kawasaki disease. Anthony's eyes, however, had shown marked improvement. In fact, there was no indication of redness and the swelling was nearly gone. Same with his tongue. "Strawberry tongue" was common with children with Kawasaki disease. His tongue was a normal, healthy pink. Same with his hands and feet, which had earlier developed severe erythema of the palms and soles, now appeared normal and healthy.

The doctor just stood there by my son's side, blinking and stammering and smiling. He was certain he was witnessing a miracle. He had—just a very different kind of miracle.

When the doctor left to order some blood work, I sat by my son's side, holding his warm hands. He continued staring at me quietly, and I was having a hard time looking him in the eye. Did he know what I had done? I didn't think so, but I suspected he knew on a very deep level. The soul level, perhaps. His outer level, the physical level, was still confused and wondering.

Finally, he spoke, and my son's little voice sounded strong. He told me he felt weird and sick to his stomach. I remember feeling sick to my stomach, too. Years ago, I had been attacked in the woods while jogging, an attack that had changed my life forever.

Why? I asked myself again. *Why attack me? For what purpose? What good was a vampire mama?*

For now, though, I comforted my son as best as I could. I asked him if he was hungry and he shook his head emphatically, his black locks whipping back and forth about his forehead. I really needed to get him a haircut.

I told him to rest. He nodded and I hugged him tightly and did my best to ignore the guilt that gripped my heart. Six years ago, after my attack, I had slept often throughout those first four days. Perhaps the length of time necessary for the body to fully assimilate the vampire blood, for the transformation to be complete. I didn't know.

Anthony would be sleeping often for the next four days, and for that I was thankful. After all, I was going to be busy looking for answers. And since his health was now assured, I felt free to leave his side.

I gave him a kiss on his cooling forehead just as he was drifting off to sleep. I got up from his side and closed the curtains tight, and slipped out of the room and out of the hospital and headed for my minivan.

I checked my watch as I stepped in. Two hours before sunlight.

As I started my vehicle, I made a call to the only other vampire in the world that I knew.

9.

I was at Detective Hanner's home in Fullerton.

The home was located in the hills above the city, and as we sat together on her second-story deck, she pointed out the rooftop of another home, barely distinguishable among a copse of thick trees. According to Hanner, the old man there was a Kabbalistic grandmaster, and was considered by many to be immortal himself.

"Then again," said Detective Hanner, crossing her bare legs and flashing me a grin, "neighbors do tend to talk."

"What, exactly, is a Kabbalistic grandmaster?"

"One who has mastered the nuances of the Kabbalah, the esoteric Jewish doctrine that facilitates a deeper connection with the great unknown, helps one gain a profound understanding of other realities and illuminates the meaning of life." Hanner turned her face toward me and I was struck again by the wildness of her eyes. They belonged to something untamed and free and hungry, a puma hunting at night, a tiger hunting in the jungles, a lion tracking its prey across the Serengeti. She grinned fiercely and added, "Or something like that."

Hanner, who had known about my plans to help my son, did not know about the medallion. Wrong or not, I trusted my new friend, and so I told her about it, and about what I needed: answers to unlocking its secret.

"Where did you get the medallion, Sam?"

"From the vampire who attacked me."

"Amazing. Others have been looking for it for a very long time. Others like us."

"There are that many who seek to end their lives?" I asked, confused.

She shrugged. "Or there are others who seek to end the lives of other immortals."

"I don't understand," I said.

"There are some immortals who are so old, so powerful, that they cannot be killed by any means, Sam."

"And the medallion could kill them?"

"Perhaps. That's the theory at least."

I shook my head, amazed all over again. "I just want my son returned to me."

Pain flashed briefly over her face, and although

her thoughts were impenetrable to me and her aura was non-existent, I was still a mother and an investigator and I could read her like a book. She was thinking of the loss of her own son who had died years ago.

Tears filled her eyes and, perhaps embarrassed, she changed the subject. "You must be famished," she said, standing.

I was. I hadn't eaten tonight and it was hitting me hard. Not to mention I had given copious amounts of my own blood to my son.

Hanner disappeared into her impressive home, and while I waited the electrified particles of light in the sky seemed agitated and frenzied, but that could have been my imagination. Or a reflection of my own inner struggles. I was having a hard time holding onto a thought for long, before it slipped away into the ether, to be quickly replaced by an equally chaotic thought.

She mercifully appeared a few minutes later, holding two full wine goblets that were filled with anything but wine. She handed one to me, which I eagerly accepted.

The glass was warm. "Fresh blood," I said.

"Of course."

"But where?"

"I have an arrangement with a mortal, Sam. A few mortals, in fact. Most of us do. It makes our lives easier."

I nodded but was soon drinking hungrily. Hell, I nearly bit through the glass. As I drank I was aware of Hanner watching me from over her own glass, her eyes as wild as I had ever seen them. I could only imagine what my own looked like.

Like an animal. A hungry animal.

I didn't savor the blood. In fact, I barely tasted it, so quickly did it pass over my lips and down my throat and into my stomach, where it interacted on some supernatural level with my own supernatural body.

When you don't need to come up for air, one can quickly down a glass of blood, and shortly it was finished but I was hesitant to return it. After all, there was still some blood pooling in the bottom and coating the inside of the glass.

"Thank you," I said, then motioned to the empty glass. "And thank...whoever provided this."

"Oh, I will." And she said that with such enthusiasm I briefly wondered what *other* kind of arrangement she had with her donors.

The hemoglobin had an immediate effect, no doubt due to its freshness. Rarely had I drank blood so fresh and pure. Even the stuff provided by Kingsley had no doubt been days or weeks old, and stored in his refrigerator.

This was different. This was straight from the source, and it was so damn good. Unable to control myself, I tilted the bloody goblet up and waited for the last few drops to crawl down, where I eagerly lapped them up. Once done, I used the edge of my index finger to scrape the inside of the glass clean.

"I'm a ghoul," I said, embarrassed.

"No different than licking brownie batter from a whisk. At least, that's what I tell myself."

"I'll tell myself that, too, but I think I'll pretend its chocolate chip cookie dough."

She smiled and sipped her own drink much more lady-like than I had. I set my glass down and secretly wished for another.

Such a ghoul.

Hanner said, "You should consider getting your own donor, Samantha. They are terribly important. I cannot imagine what you have been feeding on these past few years."

"You don't want to know."

"No, I suppose I don't."

We were silent some more and I finally set aside the glass, which had now been completely scraped clean. I found myself idly sucking under my nail.

"You are in an interesting situation, Sam."

"I don't know if I would use the word *interesting*," I said. "*Frightening*, perhaps."

"You misunderstand," said Hanner, and not for the first time I detected an odd lilt to her voice. "I mean, you have been given an interesting choice regarding your son."

"You mean I *had* been given," I said. "I already made my choice, remember, and now I must turn him back before it's too late, before he realizes what his mother has done to him."

"You misunderstand again, so let me explain clearly: Sam, you have a chance to be with your son...forever."

Her words didn't immediately sink in, but when they did, when the full realization of them hit, I was left speechless and my mouth hanging open.

"Eternity is a long, long time, Sam. Too long to be alone. Now, you will never have to be alone. Ever..." Her voice trailed off and she looked away and somewhere in the far distance a coyote howled. At least, I think it was a coyote.

10.

I parked my minivan in front of a high, wrought-iron fence, where I sat and studied the grounds beyond. Even to my eyes, which could penetrate the darkest of nights, I couldn't see much. A long winding road that led away from the fence plunged into some deep, dark woods.

Well, as deep and dark as they got in the hills above Fullerton.

I understood Detective Hanner's heartache. I understood how much she missed her own son, but I wasn't about to sentence my own son to a lifetime of blood-drinking adolescence. Not if I could help it.

According to Detective Hanner and her neighbors, the old man's property was not only protected by a high fence but also by dark magicks. I asked her what, exactly, she meant by *dark magicks*, and she shrugged and said she was only reporting what she'd heard from her neighbors. Hanner added that she wouldn't put anything past the creepy old man who may or may not be immortal.

What the hell kind of neighborhood was this?

Except this really didn't feel like a neighborhood. Not anymore. Not out here in the dark and surrounded by trees and high fences and apparently black magicks. In fact, I felt like I was in a fairy tale. A Brothers Grimm fairytale, as twisted and dark as they come. And there was no prince waiting for me at the end of this cobblestone drive. No, only an ancient master of the black arts, who may or may not be a vampire. Who may or may not be undead.

I debated turning back, but instead I got out of the minivan and approached the gate. I could have scaled the fence easy enough, but the "protected by dark magicks" part had me a little nervous. And curious.

So what would happen if I broke in? Would a wart appear on my nose? Would a she-devil manifest in a swirl of black smoke to drag me down to hell? Would Lady Gaga apparate and give me a make-over? I shuddered. I didn't know, but now was not the time to find out.

So I did it by the book, and pushed the red intercom button above a cobwebbed touchpad. I had no sooner released my finger when I got a prompt reply.

"State your name," crackled a strongly-accented voice through a speaker.

"Samantha Moon."

The speaker crackled again. "Please turn around."

"Excuse me?"

"Turn please."

I did, turning slowly, knowing there was a camera somewhere and wondering how well my make-up was holding up.

"The left side of your neck, just below your jawline, is missing."

"Excuse me?"

"It shows up as...empty on my monitors. Are you a vampire, Samantha Moon?"

I touched the area in question, and sure enough, I had missed a spot there. Damn. "Now, what kind of question is that to ask—"

"Are you a vampire or not?"

"Perhaps we can discuss this inside, where we can have a little more pri—"

"You are alone in the woods, dear girl. Let me assure you. Again, I ask: are you a vampire or not?"

I rarely, if ever, go around blurting my super-secret identity. The man in the house, whoever he was, was obviously privy to the ways of the undead. How much so, I didn't know. But I needed help for my son and I needed it asap.

"Yes," I said. "I guess you could say I'm a vampire, although I really don't think of myself as—"

"State your reason for being here, vampire. And hurry please, you are cutting into my morning rituals."

Morning rituals? I didn't like the sound of that. I suddenly had an image of a bloody forest animal staked within a pentagram, but this wasn't a psychic hit. Just my overactive imagination. In fact, as I thought about it, I wasn't getting any psychic hits from the old man. Whoever he was, he was good at concealing his thoughts.

I said, "I'm here because I need help with my son."

"What kind of help?"

"Can we please talk inside?"

There was a long pause, and then the speaker went dead and the iron gate swung open on silent hinges. I got back into the minivan and drove through. As I did so, the iron gate shut immediately behind me.

I was a vampire, dammit. I shouldn't be afraid.

But I was.

11.

There's a reason why they don't make roads out of cobblestones anymore.

Teeth rattling and brain turning nearly to mush, I soon pulled around a massive fountain that featured three rather robust mermaids, each more endowed than the next. Men and their damned mermaids, I thought. As I turned off the minivan, I actually paused to wonder if mermaids were, in fact, true.

Hell, why not?

The house was huge, complete with massive columns and a wide portico, all befitting a man who may or may not be a human. My sixth sense was telling me to be wary. It wasn't exactly ringing off the hook, but it was letting me know that there was danger here, perhaps not necessarily of the physical kind, but...something.

I stepped out of the minivan and into the cool night air. Crickets chirped nearby and the waxing moon shone through some of the taller, ornamental evergreens that marched around the property.

The house was a massive Colonial mansion, befitting America's forefathers. Our very rich forefathers. I followed a cement path through what appeared to be crushed seashells, and then stepped up on a cement veranda, and found myself before two massive double doors. My internal warning system continued beeping steadily, neither increasing or decreasing. Nothing would harm me here, I was sure, but I was being warned to stay alert and cautious.

No problem with that.

I pressed a doorbell button inlaid within an ornate brass fixture that seemed about right for a house this gaudy. A gong resonated from seemingly everywhere, followed shortly by footsteps on a wooden floor. Soon, the right door swung open and I was greeted by a wide-shouldered man with a red nose, holding a tissue. He studied me briefly, eying me along his red nose, which could have used another wipe or two, but that was probably just the mother in me. He was balding and what few stray hairs he had were wildly askew. Was he the butler? I didn't know, but I suspected so. My only experience with butlers was with Franklin, Kingsley's wildly disproportionate butler.

Finally, he nodded and wiped his nose—thank God—and said, "This way, madam."

And like Franklin, he didn't sound very happy about being roused to service in the middle of the night. But like a trooper he led me down hallways and around corners, past marble sculptures and fine works of art. The deeper we got, the more I realized that something was off. Something was different. Very different.

It was the energy in the house. It was moving slowly, spiraling oddly. Normally, energy zigzagged randomly, illuminating my night world nicely. But this energy spiraled in seemingly slow motion, as if the very house itself had slipped out of the normal flow of time. And the particles themselves blazed in multiple colors of oranges and blues and violets.

What the hell?

I stopped and stared, feeling like a teenager at her first laser light show, minus the funny mushrooms.

"This way," said the butler, and I followed him deeper into the house.

12.

The man looked like a gnome or something out of Xanth.

But it was hard to tell, since he was sitting cross-legged on a cushioned mat in the center of an empty room. I saw that a similar cushion had been placed before him. Was that for me?

He was wearing a white robe and a peaceful expression. He wasn't a vampire, I knew, because I could see his aura around him, and I was getting minor psychic hits, too, which is not the case when I'm in the presence of Detective Hanner. And it hadn't been the case when I had faced off with Captain Jack, whose mind had been completely closed to me.

But that wasn't the case here.

As I stood in the doorway, I began picking up on some fairly random thoughts. Almost as if someone were switching the channels to a radio. But no, not quite. These thoughts were on a loop, repeating over and over.

What the hell was going on? I focused on the words, trying to make sense of them, but couldn't:

"Tread carefully," came one repeated phrase. "The Great Cosmic Law is unerring," came another, and "Life is a continuous circle," and, "You cannot give without receiving, and cannot receive without giving." And still more, "Thine evil returns to thee, with still more of its kind," "Here be monsters," and others that were far stranger and completely incoherent. At least, incoherent to me, such as: "Thus humidity or water is the body, the vehicle and tool, but the spirit or fire is the operator, the universal agent and fabricator of all natural things."

They were esoteric sayings, surely. Spiritual sayings. The kind of sayings that might randomly flit through a highly-evolved mind. Or one who practiced the Kabbalah.

But the words, repeated over and over, created a sort of buzz. A white noise that was almost deafening, to the point where I was having a hard time thinking, or hearing my own thoughts.

"Please sit down, young lady," said the little man, motioning to the cushion before him. I noticed he didn't open his eyes. "At least, I assume you're young. With vampires, you just never know."

The air in the room was filled with more of the

swirling, colorful particles; somehow, these particles were moving even slower in this room.

"I'm fine right here," I said.

He nodded. "Forgive the voices you might be hearing; that is, if you can hear them. Not all creatures of the night possess this skill."

"What...what are the voices?" I asked.

He cracked a smile, although he still hadn't opened his eyes. "Ah, you can hear them. Very interesting. Yes, the voices are my defense."

"I don't understand."

"You see, it is impossible to close off your thoughts to a vampire, especially a powerful vampire, but one can provide a sort of 'white noise.' Clutter, if you will."

I nodded as if I understood—which, disturbingly, I think I did.

The old man continued, "Of course, I cannot penetrate your thoughts; at least, not yet. Not until we've developed a deeper bond or relationship, and I don't see that happening unless you have an unflagging desire to become chums with a very old man."

I smiled despite the strangeness of the situation.

"How old?" I asked.

"Old enough not to answer that question. Anyway, I will not bother to ask how you came to find me, as I'm generally always found by your kind. Indeed, the how is not important. It is the why that I'm after. *Why* are you here?"

"I need help with my son."

He smiled again. "A vampire with children?"

"Yes."

"Tragic," he said, making small noises and shaking his head.

"Why?"

"Because you will inevitably outlive your son, only to spend an eternity being barren."

"Barren?"

"Vampirism is the ultimate contraceptive."

I hadn't thought about having more kids. I hadn't realized that I would never, ever have children again. My heart sank. No wonder Hanner was so distraught.

"Ah, I see that this is news to you," he said, and still he had not opened his eyes.

I nodded. "Yes."

"You can see, then, the tragedy. There is but one way to overcome this, of course."

I suddenly knew the way, because despite his looping gibberish that filled my thoughts, I had caught a quick glance into his mind.

"Yes," I said. "The medallion."

His eyes shot open.

13.

He said nothing at first, but I saw the suspicion on his face, especially in his strange eyes, eyes that seemed devoid of color. I knew he was wondering if I had read his thoughts, or if I had simply made a supposition based on his last statement.

"What about the medallion, my dear?" he asked. He closed his eyes again, and it was just as well since his colorless irises were creepy as hell.

I told him about my son, opening up to the strange man and telling him secrets that I told few mortals. He might hold the answers to my son's return to mortality, and that was enough to keep me talking, to keep me babbling until I finally caught him up to date.

As I spoke, he sat quietly, no doubt watching

me in ways that I couldn't quite fathom. When I was finished, he said, "You have spared your son from death. Is that not the goal of most parents?"

"The goal of most parents is *not* to turn their children into blood-sucking fiends."

He nodded. "So you've turned your son, and now you wish to turn him back?"

"Yes."

"You are playing God, Samantha. Granting immortality and then taking it away."

"I'm using the tools I've been given to save my son. No more, no less."

He nodded. "The medallion. Is it in your possession?"

"It is somewhere safe."

"And you seek to unlock its secret?"

"I seek to give my son a normal life."

"Normal lives are overrated."

The energy in the room had shifted a little. It was moving a fraction faster. I think my own anger and frustration was charging the room. The old man continued sitting still, while his looping white noise continued filling my brain. What kind of secrets was he keeping from me? Perhaps it was better that I didn't know.

"I do not have strength to argue the point," he said. "Keeping you out of my thoughts is highly taxing. Tell me, what exactly can I do for you?"

"I need help in unlocking the medallion."

"And reversing your son's vampirism?"

"Yes."

He sat quietly. He was tiring. The whispery phrases that cluttered my thoughts seemed to be faltering, skipping words here and there. His defense was breaking down, and I idly wondered what mysteries might be lurking in his brain.

"There is a way, of course," he said. "There's always a way. But for my services I always require payment."

My eyes narrowed. Any woman's eyes would narrow when she hears a creepy old man utter the words: *I require payment.*

"What kind of payment?" I asked warily.

"Life, of course."

"What does that mean?"

"It means that for my service I require life, usually in the form of years removed from yours and added to mine."

So he was a vampire, after all. Or a type of vampire. One that sucked life, not blood, no doubt through the use of arcane magicks.

He went on, "But you have no years to remove, my dear, being immortal. To remove years implies that one's life has an ending point." He opened his eyes and looked directly at me. "You, lass, will live forever, if you are lucky."

Indeed. For creatures who are immortal, we tend to die easily enough if we find ourselves on the wrong end of a silver dagger.

My eyes narrowed. "So what are you getting at?"

"Your son's life, of course, Samantha. For my

help, I require three years from your son's life, that is, of course, if you are successful in your bid to return him to his mortality."

"How will this be done?"

"Delicately, my dear. Your son will not be harmed."

I felt sick all over again. Jesus, what had I gotten Anthony involved with? "He will lose three years of his life?"

He opened his eyes again and now that his psychic shell was cracking, I saw something monstrous about the man. A darkness appeared around him, swirled briefly, and then disappeared again. The man was possessed by something dark. Of that I was sure. Something that required the years of the living to sustain it.

"Or your son can live forever," he said. "The choice is yours, my dear."

The air in the room had grown agitated. The calm, beautiful lights had been replaced by crazed, dancing butterflies of all colors.

"And what are you offering me in return? Do you know how to unlock the medallion?"

"I know of one who does. An alchemist older than even me."

"So you are not a vampire?"

He grinned wickedly. "No. At least, not the blood sucking kind."

"And that's all you're offering me? The name of an alchemist for three years of my son's life?"

"Yes."

"And what, exactly, does that mean? Three years of his life?"

"Your son's life, should he become mortal again, will be cut short by three years. Years which will then be transferred to me."

"You're sick."

"No," he breathed. "I'm *alive*, as I plan on being for many years to come."

He explained further: my son's life would not necessarily end tragically. It would simply end as it was meant to end, only three years earlier.

Lord help me.

"Where do I find this guy?"

"I know not, my dear. In fact, no one knows. And those who have seen him claim that *he* has found *them*."

Great. I closed my eyes and took in a lot of air, and held it for seemingly an eternity. "One year," I finally said.

"Three!" he hissed angrily.

Sweet Jesus. I was bargaining with my son's life. His years. "One," I said. "Only one."

"Two," he screeched. "Two! And no less!"

"Okay," I said weakly. "Two."

He clapped his hands thunderously. "Then it is done!"

14.

Before crawling into bed, I called the hospital. According to the doctor on staff, Anthony was sleeping quietly and showing signs of marked improvement. I could hear the relief in his voice.

I thanked him for everything and hung up. My daughter, I knew, was with my sister. I was alone and exhausted. My body was shutting down. I sent texts to Danny and my sister, too weak to call. I told them the good news, that Anthony was miraculously recovering. I didn't explain the miraculous part. I hoped I would never have to, either. I told my sister to tell Tammy that I loved her, then set my alarm for noon. I had just slipped into bed when I felt the sun rise, felt it in every fiber of my being.

Oh, what a night.

And just before blackness overcame me, I thought of the name I had been given.

Archibald Maximus.

***

I awoke sluggishly, reluctantly, painfully.

During the day, I felt mortal. During the day, I felt less than human. I dragged my tired ass out of bed, hopped in the shower, where I stood under the scalding hot spray until I used up all the hot water. In the bathroom mirror, other than a few beads of water that seemed to be floating in mid-air, I saw nothing. Neither follicle nor fingernail.

Nothing.

How is that possible? What the hell is happening?

My son would see nothing, too. Forever nothing, unless I found him a cure. And with that thought, as I gazed at nothing in the mirror, I realized that I would forever be undead.

Forever.

Jesus.

Recently, I had held out hope that I might someday use the medallion for myself, the thought never occurring to me that I would need it for my son instead.

An eternity on this earth.

Alone.

I continued standing before the empty mirror,

dripping on the bathroom floor. I looked down at the puddle forming below me...there was no reflection there either.

I don't exist, I thought.

Panic gripped me. It had been quite a while since I had had a full-blown panic attack, but I was close to having one now. I circled the bathroom, slipping in the puddle once. There was no image pacing alongside of me in the bathroom mirror. Nothing.

Not seeing yourself in a mirror, or window, or fucking puddle has a way of playing on one's nerves. And my nerves were shot.

Completely fucking shot.

I circled, breathing deeply, trying to calm myself, until I realized that breathing deeply didn't calm me. Breathing deeply didn't do *shit.*

I broke out in a sweat.

Maybe I really don't exist. It's a fear I've had over the years. A fear that I was still back in the hospital, recovering from my attacks so many years ago. In a coma. Or worse. Maybe I was dead. Maybe all of this is happening in my dead mind. Was that even possible?

I continued sweating, continued pacing in the bathroom. I looked to my right, in the mirror. Nothing except a ghostly, wet outline of a curvy woman.

That's just not right. That's just fucked up. I mean, who can't see themselves in mirrors?

Vampires can't, Sam. Vampires.

Calm down. Relax. You're okay. You're here. You're really here.

Naked and still dripping, I found myself in my living room, at my house phone. I called the only number I trusted to call. My sister Mary Lou answered immediately.

"Hi, love!" she said excitedly. "I've been waiting for you to wake up. Such great news about Anthony!"

I agreed and her excitement buoyed me, but I was far from better. I was far from thinking reasonably. A great panic had taken hold and I was a woman drowning in her own fear.

"Mary Lou," I said, and her name caught in my throat.

"Sam? Is everything okay?"

"Mary Lou, I don't understand."

"Understand what?"

I tried again, my mind racing, my heart beating faster than it had in quite some time. "Mary Lou, is this really happening?"

"What do you mean, Sam?"

I started crying, so hard that I could barely hold the phone. I was losing it. You would, too. Anyone would. Trust me, there's only so much a person can take. "Am I really here, Mary Lou...please...I need to know. Is this real? Is this really happening to me?"

"Is this about Anthony? But he's okay, Sam. He's—"

"No. It's not about Anthony. Please, Louie.

Please."

"What do you need, Sam? What is it?"

"I don't understand what's happened to me, Louie."

"Oh, honey...sweetie..."

I wept harder than I had wept in a long, long time. I sank to my knees. It took a full minute before I could speak again. "Is this all a dream, Louie?"

"It's not a dream, honey. This is real. Everything's real."

I thought of the empty mirror and shook my head even though my sister couldn't see me shaking my head.

"No, it can't be. It's impossible."

"Honey, listen to me. Something very bad happened to you, but you're going to be okay. I promise. And now Anthony's going to be okay, too."

I thought of Anthony and what I had done to him, and found myself sobbing nearly hysterically. The last words I heard from my sister was that she was coming right over.

15.

My sister is one of the few people on earth who know about my "condition."

I have other family members, of course. A sister in San Francisco, a brother in New York, and my parents in the high desert, but I was not close to them. My sister, Mary Lou, and I had always been more like twins, even though she was six years older than me. Back when I was attacked and left for dead—or, more accurately, left for *eternity*—it had been Mary Lou who was by my side. In fact, I didn't even receive a phone call from my brother until three days later.

It's hard to forget something like that.

Mary Lou and I will probably never live very far apart. She is my rock. Men come and go, friends come and go, but my sister will always be there for me.

That I would someday outlive her is a very real possibility. That I would watch my sister steadily grow old and wither is a very real possibility. Somehow, this was less difficult to accept than watching my own kids grow into old age.

Of course, if I failed to unlock the secrets of the medallion, I wouldn't have to worry about this with Anthony.

Panic gripped me.

Calm down, Samantha. Be calm. You're of no use to anyone if you're panicking.

As I waited for my sister, sitting there with my back against the living room wall, sitting between an end table and a bookcase, I realized that I didn't know what the hell I was doing. What if unlocking the medallion somehow hurt Anthony? What if the process of returning him to his mortality was painful? What if something went wrong?

Oh, Jesus...what have I done?

"You saved him," I whispered to myself, hugging my knees and rocking. "You saved him. That's what you did. Now just fix it, Sam. *Fix it.*"

A car pulled up outside and soon I heard feet rapidly approaching. My sister was using her own key to unlock the door and soon she was inside and in the living room and on the ground next to me, holding me closely, and crying with me.

God, I loved my sister.

But she had no idea why I was crying, and I

would not tell her, not ever. Not if I didn't have to.

"C'mon," she said, hauling me to my feet. "Let's go see Anthony."

"Where's Tammy?"

"Rick's watching her and the kids."

"Rick's a good man."

"The best. Now, let's get you dressed..."

16.

At the hospital, we found Anthony asleep. No surprise there, since it was the middle of the day.

With guilt nearly overwhelming me, I listened to the doctor express his concern over my son's slower than normal heartbeat, a condition he called *bradycardia*, which apparently could lead to a cardiac arrest. My sister looked increasingly concerned about this news, but I held my poise. The slowing of my son's heart rate was to be expected, after all. Expected by me, at least. Hell, my own heart barely beat a few times a minute.

Other than the decreasing heartbeat, everything looked good and, according to the doctor, if my son kept up this healing pace, he might even be released in a few days.

Good news, surely, for any mother. Mary Lou hugged me tightly and I felt her tears on my face. She pulled away and wiped her eyes and was unaware of a very different expression on my face.

I could not predict how I looked, but I suspected it was a look of desperation. After all, I had three and a half days by my reckoning to unlock the secret to the medallion.

Or my son would forever stay a vampire.

At age seven.

Sweet Jesus.

I asked Mary Lou if she would stay with Anthony for a few hours while I took care of some business. She said of course, and as she pulled up a chair, she took out a black and narrow device that looked suspiciously like one of those Kindle thingies.

She powered it on, settled in, and I headed out.

Maybe I should get one of those someday.

17.

In my minivan, with my specialized window shades drawn tight, I Googled *Archibald Maximus* on my iPhone, a device that was quickly becoming the private investigator's greatest tool.

Nothing of note.

I tried the name without the quotes, including other possible related keywords:

Archibald Maximus, vampire. Although a ton of sites popped up, very few were even close to what I was looking for. And the few that were turned out to be either porn or dead ends.

Archibald Maximus, medallion. Same thing. Nothing.

Archibald Maximus, alchemist. Nothing.

Archibald Maximus, wizard. Nothing. Wait!

Something. No, never mind. Just another porn site.

I really hadn't expected an obscure alchemist to have a web page or even a Twitter account, although that would have certainly made my job easier.

I next tried the name in my various industry databases, sites that only private investigators have access to. Nothing. Not even an unlikely hit. Whoever Archibald Maximus was, he didn't own property, have a criminal record in the United States, nor had he applied for credit.

I next called my ex-partner at HUD, Chad Helling. He answered on the second ring, which made me feel good.

"Good morning, Sunshine."

"Never gets old does it?" I was referring to his nickname for me. *Sunshine.* In Chad Helling's simple world, the nickname was supposed to be ironic. And funny.

"Not yet," he said, chuckling.

"You need to get a life."

"I'm working on it," he said. "I'm going to ask her, Sam."

"Ask her what? And who?"

"Monica. I'm going to ask her to marry me."

I shook my head. The poor dope. "Isn't it a little too soon?"

"For love? Never!"

Oh, brother. "Listen, Romeo, I've got a job for you."

"Paying work?"

"Sure," I said. "A coffee and a scone."

"The coffee I'll take. I'm still not sure what the hell a scone is."

I gave him the name and asked him to use the agency's database.

"Archibald Maximus?" he asked, confirming.

"Yes."

"What is he, a wrestler or something?"

"Maybe."

"Really?"

"No."

Chad grumbled something about doing my work for me and told me he would get back to me as soon as he had something.

I was still in the hospital parking lot, parked under a pathetic-looking tree, whose branches only provided me with partial shade. The minivan was heating up and by all rights I should crack the windows and let in some fresh air. Except, I didn't need fresh air, and so I didn't bother. Cracked windows let in sunlight, and sunlight was far more detrimental to me than stale air. Also, there wasn't a car on earth that could heat up hot enough to remove the eternal cold from my bones. In fact, I craved the heat, and so I sat in the minivan, baking, breathing stale air, and thinking hard.

I had only one answer.

I reached into my purse and removed the small legal pad I now kept tucked in a side pocket. I also removed a favorite pen with flowing, liquid black ink. I love flowing, liquid black ink.

As a small wind rushed over the van, swishing the tree above and scattering a few precious leaves from its sparse branches, I spent the next few minutes going through a meditation exercise that both grounded me to the earth and opened me to the spirit world.

Once grounded and open, I sat quietly with pen in hand, waiting. Shortly, I felt the familiar tingle in my right arm. The tingle turned into something more than a tingle. In fact, it turned into an electrical impulse and my right arm involuntarily spasmed. It spasmed again and again, lightly, and soon the pen in my hand was moving, seemingly on its own. Writing. Two words appeared on the mini-sheet of legal paper before me.

Hello, Samantha.

"Hello," I said within the empty minivan, feeling slightly silly.

In the past, two different entities had come through in this form of communication, what many call "automatic writing." I asked now who I was speaking with. My hand twitched once, twice, and the name *Sephora* appeared before me. Sephora, I knew, was my personal spirit guide.

Whatever the hell that was.

"I might have done a bad thing," I said.

My hand jerked and spasmed and more words appeared on the notepad on my lap.

You are only as bad as you feel, Samantha.

"Well, I feel like shit and I'm scared to death."

My hand flinched rapidly.

Did you act out of love or fear when you saved your son?

I thought hard about that. Sweat was now breaking out on my brow. It took a lot for sweat to break out on my brow. The car was heating up rapidly. "I acted out of instinct," I said. "For me, it was the only answer. I had a means to save my son, and I took it. Some would call that love, others would call it selfishness."

The electrical impulse crackled through my arm.

What would you call it, Samantha?

"Love. It has to be. I love my kids more than anything."

Then so be it.

Interestingly, had I not possessed the medallion, I don't think I would have done it. In fact, I *know* I wouldn't have done it. I would not have sentenced my son to...*this*...if there was no way to turn him back.

"Does my son know what's happened to him?" I asked.

Your son sleeps deeply while the change comes over him. In the physical, outer world, no. But, yes, his greater self, his soul self, knows exactly what you have done.

"Does he forgive me?"

My child, he loves you with all his heart. He understands this was a difficult decision for you, and that you made the best choice you could.

I stared down at the words on the pad, wondering again if I was making them up or if they were really flowing through me from the spirit world.

"You make it seem like there's two of him," I said.

There is his higher, spiritual self, Samantha, and his lower, physical self. The higher self resides in the spirit world, and the lower self in the physical world, your world.

I thought about that, then got to why I was here. "I have a name of a man who might be able to help me," I said.

There was no response. No weird electrical impulse. My arm rested lightly on the center console.

"Is there a way you can help me find him?"

Precious child, there is always a way. To find what is missing, lost or hidden, requires great faith, patience and perseverance.

I waited, but apparently that's all I was going to be given.

"Is that it?" I asked.

It is enough, Samantha.

I slammed the pen down and tore out the sheet of paper. A few seconds later, the paper was nothing more than confetti. I knew I was acting like a baby. Losing control was exactly what I *shouldn't* be doing. But I didn't need riddles and spiritual platitudes. I needed Archibald Maximus.

And I needed him now.

18.

The only other vampire I knew—outside of my newly anointed son—had led me to the world's creepiest man, which cost my son two years of his life. As shitty as that sounded, a name had been gleaned, which was more than I started with.

The only other immortal that I knew was Kingsley Fulcrum, a beast of a man in more ways than one. He had an office a block or two from the hospital, across the street from the opulent Main Place Mall, which I was driving past now. The mall gleamed and sparkled and apparently emitted a siren call to Orange County housewives everywhere.

I somehow managed to ignore the call, and soon I was turning into the parking lot of Kingsley's plush, red-brick office building, which brought to mind the last time I was here.

Last week, I had stormed into Kingsley's office, scaring off a wife killer that Kingsley had been set to represent. Exactly. I'd never been more proud. Anyway, the last I heard Kingsley had dropped the piece of shit. Unfortunately for the killer, I had gotten a very strong psychic hit from him. I knew, without a doubt, that he had killed his wife. Now he was on my radar, and I intended to follow through with my threat to make sure that he spent a lifetime in prison.

But that was for another time. For now, I had a son to save.

From what? I asked myself. *From an eternity of life? From an eternity of not experiencing death?*

No, I answered. *From an eternity of childhood. From an eternity of consuming blood. From an eternity of questioning his sanity.*

It was mid-day and I was at my weakest and frailest. I also felt vulnerable and clumsy. As I stood there on the bottom floor, inside the glass doors, blinking and waiting for my eyes to adjust to the gloom within, I realized something else. I had condemned my son to a lifetime of shunning the sun.

My son would never again go to the beach, never again go on a field trip with his class, never again play Frisbee in the park. Granted, he never played Frisbee in the park, anyway, but that possibility had been removed.

For now, I thought. *Only for now. There is an answer. There has to be an answer.*

I moved heavily through the building, all too aware that my legs felt unusually heavy, that each step was an effort, that I did not belong with the day dwellers.

A tall man wearing an outdated blue blazer smiled at me sadly as I boarded the elevator. He asked what floor and I noticed we were going to the same floor, Kingsley's floor. As we rode up together, I touched my brow and winced. Despite my wide-brimmed hat, some of the sun had made it through. There might have been a small area near my hairline where I had missed some sunblock because the skin there was burning. I ignored the pain, knowing it would go away in a few hours.

We rode the elevator in silence. I was aware of the man in the old business suit watching me. I hated to be watched and self-consciously moved away, ducking my head, wishing like hell he would look away, but too weak to do anything other than shrink away like a frightened puppy.

"Pardon me," he said in a thick French accent, leaning in front of me and pushing the button to the floor just beneath Kingsley's offices. "Wrong floor."

The elevator doors opened immediately, and he stepped out. As he did so, he turned and looked at me again. He was a tall man wearing a bow tie. I hadn't noticed the bow tie before. His age was indeterminate, anything from 48 to 78. Then he did something that shocked the hell out of me.

He smiled.

The elevator doors closed and I headed up to see Kingsley.

19.

Like I said, the last time I was here, I stormed Kingsley's office like a mad woman.

Or a desperate mom.

This time I waited patiently in the lobby while Kingsley finished up with a client. Oh, I was still desperate. I was still driven. It's just that I had eased up on the panic button. A few days ago, when I had stormed in here, my son was close to death. Now he was very much alive, although I was faced with a whole new dilemma.

Had I been anything less than what I am now, my son, I knew, would be dead. He would have fulfilled his life mission, a mission that included checking out early, apparently, and the rest of us would have been left to pick up the pieces of our own lives, if that was even possible.

There were a lot of unanswered questions. The use of the medallion was so vague, so strange, and just so damn weird. That I was pinning my son's eternity on a golden coin hanging from a leather strap was mind-boggling and disturbing, at best.

And what was I working so hard for? To ensure that my son *would* someday die? Where things stood, he would survive and keep surviving forever. Wasn't that a *good* thing? And how did I know that he would stop growing? Maybe he would continue to grow. Maybe he would reach adulthood. Maybe he would thank me every day for the rest of his life, for all eternity, for sparing him from death, and for giving him great physical gifts, too. Knowing my son, in the least, he would thank me for getting him out of school.

This line of thinking had me confused. Jesus, maybe I should let him be. Maybe with proper guidance, I could walk him through the eternal experience, help him, teach him, guide him. Something no one had done for me. Maybe he would indeed grow into his adult body.

Maybe.

Or maybe not.

I didn't know; I knew so little.

Shit.

A few minutes later, Kingsley's office door opened and out came a familiar client. The same client I had seen just days earlier. The same client who had prompted a powerful vision of him strangling his wife to death in her sleep. The same coward. The same piece of shit. The same asshole I had threatened to bring down.

It was no threat.

And here he was. Coming out of Kingsley's office.

Again.

We locked eyes and I think we both gasped. My stomach heaved at the sight of the bastard. He made a small, whimpering sound and took a step back...into Kingsley, who was standing behind him. Kingsley looked surprised, too. He also looked a little sheepish and embarrassed. I was too stunned to speak.

Kingsley quickly stepped between us, and actually escorted the bastard out of his office. A moment later, my werewolf friend returned, all six foot, six inches of him, and gestured toward his office.

"Let's talk," he said.

Numb and sick, I silently stood and headed through his open door.

He followed behind, shutting the door.

"Have a seat," he said.

20.

I did as I was told, still too stunned to speak.

Kingsley moved around his office with an ease and speed uncommon for a man his size. He sat in his executive chair and studied me for a long moment before speaking. I could not look into his eyes.

"Well, I suppose I should thank you for not playing Whack-A-Mole with my client's head," he finally said, and I could hear the gentle humor in his voice. He was referring to an inadvertent joke he'd made the other day.

I didn't smile. Not now.

He took in a lot of air. Unlike me, Kingsley seemed to need normal amounts of oxygen. I know this because I had listened to him snore once or twice. *Listene*d, of course, was putting it mildly. *Experienced*, perhaps? His snoring was unlike anything I had ever heard before. It sounded like the bombing of a small village.

He filled his massive chest to capacity, which put a lot of pressure on his nice dress shirt, especially the buttons. I was prepared to duck should buttons start flying like so many bullets from a Gatling gun.

He studied me like that for a moment, his chest filled, button threads hanging on for dear life, and then finally expelled. He leaned back and crossed his legs, adjusting the drape of his hem.

"Don't judge me, Sam," he said. I noticed he looked away when he spoke.

"Who's judging?" I said. "I'm just admiring the fine handiwork of your shirt."

"Every man deserves a fair trial, Sam."

"And every defense attorney deserves a hefty payday."

"This has nothing to do with money, Sam."

"Say that to your mansion in Yorba Linda."

"My home is the result of a lot of hard work."

"And a lot of freed killers."

Perhaps in frustration, he closed both hands into boulder-like fists, and as he did so, his knuckles cracked mightily. Jesus, he was an intimidating son-of-a-bitch, but I was not easily intimidated.

"What do you want, Sam?" he asked.

I found myself wanting to lash out, too. I found myself wanting to storm out and flip him the bird.

How...how could a man represent such scum? And how could I ever respect such a man?

The answer was easy: I couldn't.

I continued saying nothing. I just sat there, battling my emotions, knowing that Kingsley might be the only person I knew who could help me find Archibald Maximus, but hating that I needed his help.

And in my silence, Kingsley must have spotted something. His thick eyebrows knitted and he sat forward a little. "Unbelievable," he said.

"What?"

"You did it, didn't you?"

"Did what?" But I knew what he was talking about. Kingsley was closed to me, as were all immortals, apparently, but we both were experts in reading body language.

"You turned him, Sam, didn't you?"

"I saved him."

He looked away, shaking his great head. "And *you* have the nerve to come in here and accuse *me* of being selfish. You, who condemned your own son to an eternity of childhood."

"What was I supposed to do, goddammit? Watch him die?"

"There's a natural order to things, Sam."

"And we're not natural?"

"No, we're not."

"And part of that natural order is to let my son die?"

He said nothing, but I saw his brain working.

The great attorney was looking for a counter-argument, but I would be damned if I was going to listen to an argument *for* my son's death.

"Look," I said. "I don't know much about much, but I know one thing: I'm a mother first. I am a mother and that is my baby in the hospital. He was sick and I had an answer. It might not have been the best answer, and I sure as hell don't expect to win any 'Mother of the Year' awards. I also don't understand what the hell happened to me, or what the hell even happened to you. I have no clue the power and magicks behind what keeps us alive. But if this fucking curse, this disease, that I live with every day can somehow save my son, somehow keep my life from spinning completely and totally out of fucking control, you damn well better believe I'm going to utilize it, because it sure as hell has taken a lot from me, Kingsley."

He was nodding. "Okay, now that you've justified turning your son into a blood-sucking fiend, what are you going to do now?"

"I'm going to find someone who can help me."

"Help you how? With the medallion?"

"Yes. I have a name."

"Where did you get the name?"

"It doesn't matter," I said, and debated storming out of the office. Instead, I kept my ego in check for my son. "Have you ever heard of someone named Archibald Maximus?"

There was no recognition on his face. "No," he said. "You don't forget a name like that."

"Do you know anyone who could help me?"

"I pointed you to the only person I knew who could help you," he said.

That had been Detective Hanner. I sensed Kingsley's hesitation. Did he know someone else? I sensed that he might, but he didn't say anything else. Instead, he was now looking at me like I was the biggest piece of shit he'd ever seen. Probably with the same expression I had been wearing just a few minutes earlier.

"I don't know who else to turn to," I said, biting the bullet. "I know you don't agree with what I've done. Quite frankly, I don't agree with a lot of what you've done, either. But let's put aside our differences for now, okay? I made the best choice I could. I did what I thought was right. There's a chance, a very small chance, that I can return my son to mortality without any lasting repercussion or effects. But if I hadn't done what I did, there was a hundred percent chance that I was going to lose my son. I gave him a chance at life, Kingsley. Was it selfish for me to keep my little boy alive and expose him to something he never asked for? Yes, it was. I agree. I'm horrible. But my son is alive, and there is a chance to return things to normal. Normal is all I'm asking for, Kingsley. Please help me."

He looked at me for a long moment, and the fact that he had to decide whether or not to help me, crushed my heart almost completely. I didn't want a man who had to decide whether or not to help me, even if he didn't agree with my choices.

Finally, he sighed and nodded, and said, "I'll see what I can do, Sam. But I make no promises."

I smiled even as my heart broke. "Thank you, Kingsley."

As I left his office, Kingsley wouldn't look at me. I said goodbye and he merely nodded. If I was a betting woman, I would bet that our relationship was over.

Forever.

21.

I was driving north on the 57 Freeway.

I checked with my sister and my son was still sleeping contentedly. The doctors seemed pleased that he was stable, but there was still mild concern, most notably that his body temperature had now dropped to 97 degrees, one degree lower than normal.

This didn't worry me. My son was going to make it, and the doctors were going to have a conundrum on their hands, much as they had with me, in a different hospital, over six years ago.

My sister asked what I was up to, and I told her that it was a very important case, a matter of life and death. She understood, but just barely. Her husband, who was watching Tammy and her kids, would be picking her up soon. I made it a point to be there when the sun set.

After all, tonight would be my son's first night as...something far different than he was before.

I exited on Orangethorpe and worked my way over to Hero's in Fullerton. I checked the time. Fang should just be showing up to work. I was right.

As I dashed in from the blistering heat, gasping and clutching my chest, I saw the tall bartender doing something very unbartender-like. He was texting. Just as I stepped into the bar, my cell phone chimed.

I paused just inside the doorway and fished out the cell. It was a text, of course, from Fang. It read: *Good afternoon, Moon Dance, how are you?*

I wrote: *I could say I'm fine, but that would be a lie. By the way, the guy at the end of the bar needs another beer, so quit texting and start working.*

I hit send and waited.

Fang had just spotted the guy at the end of the bar, who had just motioned him over, when his cell phone vibrated. Fang paused and read the screen, and I watched with some satisfaction from the doorway as his mouth dropped open. Then started looking around until he spotted me. I waved, and he shook his head.

"I was beginning to think you were everywhere, Moon Dance," he said.

"Is that a bad thing?"

He winked. "Not for me. Hold on." He drew the

guy a draft of beer and came back. "I think our connection is growing stronger."

"How so?" I asked.

"I was texting you as you came in."

"Could have been a coincidence, and is texting even a word?"

"If not, it should be," he said. "Anyway, there are no coincidences, Moon Dance."

I grabbed a stool at the far end of the bar. Privacy, for me, is always good. I said, "That would sound deep if it wasn't bullshit."

"Bullshit, huh? Then how do you explain that for the past half hour I've been feeling increasingly...troubled."

"Maybe you had some bad Chinese."

"Not bad Chinese, Sam. And how would you explain that I've felt incredible *grief* coming from you. Wave after wave of it. I sensed that something profound had ended."

I thought of my relationship with Kingsley. "Ended?"

He shook his head. "Crazy, I know. But, to me, I felt a finality to something, as if something emotional and tragic had ended. Of course, I assumed it was something to do with your son."

Jesus, my connection with Fang is growing. "My son is fine," I said.

He narrowed his eyes. "How fine?"

I nodded, confirming his suspicions.

His jaw dropped. "You really did it?"

I nodded again.

"And how is he?"

"He's fine. He's great, in fact."

Fang leaned on his elbows. The grisly teeth around his neck—definitely *not* shark teeth—clacked together with the sound of knuckles striking knuckles.

"But you're not fine," he said.

"My job's not over."

He nodded. "The medallion."

I caught him up to date, noting the striking difference between the way he handled the news and the way Kingsley had. There was no judgment in Fang's voice. There was only concern for me and my son.

He said, "And so the ending I felt was the end of your relationship with Kingsley."

"Maybe," I said.

"I'm sorry."

"No, you're not. I'm sure you're glad he's out of the picture."

Aaron Parker, aka Fang, shook his head. "I would not be much of a friend if I wished for you to experience pain on any level."

Now I was shaking my head. "Not as much pain as you might think. Kingsley is an amazing man, as you well know, and he was there for me when I needed him the most, but...it was bad timing. I was just dealing with the end of my marriage. I wasn't ready to start a new relationship."

"And he wanted to start one?"

"He wanted something, more than what I could

give him. But it's not that."

"It's ideological," said Fang, picking up on my thoughts. In fact, I could even *feel* him in my thoughts.

"We're just too different," I said. "Apples and oranges."

"Vampires and werewolves."

I smiled at that. Fang smiled, too, and I sensed his strong need to reach out and touch me, but he held back. One relationship had ended. Now was not the time to push for another. Perhaps not for a long, long time.

"It takes all my willpower, Sam," he said, tracing his finger along the scarred bar top in front of my hand, "to *not* touch you."

"I just need a friend," I said.

"I know," he said. "And you have one. Always."

22.

I was on my second glass of wine, even if the first one did little more than upset my stomach. I haven't had a good buzz in half a decade, and I suspected my days of being buzzed were long gone.

Being buzzed was overrated, I thought. Now, flying high over Orange County was a different story.

There are some benefits to being a creature of the night.

Fang and I got back to the subject of my son. He said, "I'm still fairly involved in the vampire online community. I'll ask around about our friend Archibald Maximus."

"You're still hanging out in chat rooms?"

"Often."

"They seem so...five years ago."

"Don't knock them, young lady. It's where I met you, after all."

Years ago, confused and lost, I had joined a vampire IM chat group hoping to learn anything I could about the undead. I hadn't expected to learn much of anything, let alone create such a deep and lasting friendship.

I said, "Well, I don't have a lot of hope."

"We'll see what turns up. Remember, you never know who might be popping into some of those chat rooms."

"Like me," I said.

"Right, like you. Sometimes I come across the real deal."

"How do you know they're the real deal?" I asked, suddenly feeling a pang of jealousy for reasons I couldn't quite understand but wasn't in the mood to probe very deeply.

"Oh, you know. I've made it my life's ambition to find vampires."

"And to be one."

Fang glanced at me sharply. Last week, the handsome freak asked me to turn him into a vampire, so that we could live together, or some cheesy crap like that. Not that I didn't believe him, but I was suspecting he would do anything— anything—to be a vampire. Fang's story was... interesting, to say the least. Interesting and disturbing. Born with a rare defect, his canine teeth had grown in exceptionally long, so long that he had lived with the "vampire" stigma during his entire adolescence and most of his teen years. Childish insults, mostly, but with such ferocity and frequency that he came to believe he was vampire.

In an act of passion and violence, his teenage girlfriend had ended up dead and Fang had gone on to have one of the most memorable trials to date. O.J. Simpson with teeth, as some called it.

Later, Fang would escape a high-security insane asylum...and kill two guards in the process. His whereabouts were presently unknown to law enforcement, a secret he had entrusted to me, much as I had entrusted one to him.

We all have our secrets.

Fang, or Aaron Parker, had never lost his passion for vampires, even when his two massive canine teeth had been gruesomely removed in the insane asylum—teeth that now hung around his neck to this day. Six years of online chatting and one bang-up job of stalking on his part later, and here we were. Friends with issues. Friends with secrets. But most important...friends.

His request had caught me off guard, and I would consider it later, but for now I could only think about my son. He understood this, of course, which wasn't hard to do since he was powerfully and psychically connected to me.

He grinned at that last line of thought. "I can think of no other person I would rather be powerfully and psychically attached to, Moon Dance," he said, using my old chat room username.

"You've been reading my thoughts," I said.

"It's not like I can help it," said Fang. "So, from what I gather, you don't find me such a bad guy."

"No," I said. "But you have your issues. Scary issues."

"I could say the same thing about you."

"Touché," I said, although I thought his comparison wasn't quite fair. I had never asked for any of this.

"And neither had I," said Fang, picking up on my thoughts.

"Victims of circumstance, you had said."

"Something like that," said Fang. "We are what we are."

"Fine," I said. "But be discreet with your inquiries."

"Of course," he said.

I thought of my son. I didn't have to check my watch to know that the sun would be setting in a few hours. I seemed chrono-kinetically attuned to the sun. Soon, Anthony would be waking up after sleeping through his first day. I wanted to be there for him.

"Chrono-kinetically?" said Fang, picking up my thoughts.

"It works," I said.

He grinned. "Hey, it just occurred to me that you might want to take a look at Cal State Fullerton's library."

"Why?"

"Apparently they've got quite an occult

department there. You know, books. Real books. With paper and dust and ink. A guy was just in here going on and on about their extensive collection."

"What guy?"

"Young guy."

"Maybe," I said, standing, leaving my wine half-finished. Always the pessimist these days.

"Where to now?" he asked.

I thought about it. I had a few hours before Anthony awakened. I said, "I need to beat the shit out of something."

23.

I was at my gym with my trainer.

By "gym" I meant my boxing studio. By "trainer" I meant the little old Irish guy named Jacky who talked like a leprechaun.

"Hands up, lass. Up, up!"

"Go to hell," I grunted, as I lifted my heavy hands. Vampire or not, I was nearly mortal during the day, and my hands felt like lead, especially after going through a few rounds on the heavy bag.

But even though sunset was still under two hours away, I had more than enough strength to hit the bag hard enough to rock the little trainer. He grunted through the shockwaves, screaming at me to keep my hands up even as he struggled to hold onto the bag.

"End round!" he shouted, just as I leveled another hard roundhouse. Unfortunately, the Irishman had let his guard down just enough. The punch, although mostly absorbed by the heavy bag, sent him staggering backwards.

"You okay, Jacky?" I cried out, moving over to him and catching him just as he stumbled over my gym bag.

As I held him up, the Irishman looked at me with eyes slightly crossed, sweat pouring down his face. A second later his eyes uncrossed and he stared at me. "Jesus, you're a freak."

"I've heard that before. From you, in fact."

But he was still staring at me. "And how did you get over here so fast?"

"What can I say? Cat-like reflexes."

"Freak-like reflexes," he said in his Irish trill. "I need a break, Sam."

He took his break, and in his office, through his partially open door, I saw him down a few cups of water and what looked like pain medication. He came back, cracked his neck, grabbed the heavy bag from behind, and said, "Round four. Let's do this."

And we did this, with Jacky grunting and taking the brunt of the impacts and screaming at me to keep my hands up. I cursed and punched and did my best to keep my hands up, and all the while I felt the sun slipping slowly toward the horizon.

24.

A quick shower and a few miles later and I was at the Cal State Fullerton library, which was bigger than I remembered.

I had graduated here in my early twenties with a degree in criminal justice. That degree led to a job interview with the Department of Housing and Urban Development, where I was eventually hired as a federal agent. A great job, and one I regretted leaving, but it's hard to work the day shift when you're a creature of the night.

The Cal State Fullerton library was epic. Granted, I've never been to other university libraries but I would be hard-pressed to believe any of them could be as big as this one. There were five floors of books, with rows upon rows of aisles that seemed endless. Cubicles everywhere, filled with students connected to iPods, iPhones and iEverything else. The juxtaposition of dusty library with modern technology was striking. Two worlds colliding.

At the information desk, I found a terminal and punched in the name "Archibald Maximus." Or tried to. Typing with these sharp nails was a bitch. A few tries later and I hit "enter" with little hope.

I wasn't surprised. As expected, nothing came up.

I thought about what Fang had said about the university having a considerable occult section and decided to ask someone about it.

That someone turned out to be a flirty young man with a killer smile. He was standing behind a long, curved desk, stacking books.

"Where might I find your occult section?" I asked.

He blinked. "The Occult Reading Room?" Some of the flirt left him. Just some.

I nodded encouraging, and his grin returned and I could see his mind trying to find some angle to use for a come-on line. He found none, and seemed disappointed with himself. That is, if his long sigh was any indication.

"Third floor," he said. "And you're in luck. The room's only open two hours a day and you have about twenty minutes."

"Lucky me," I said, turning. "Thank you."

"I can show it to you, if you like—"

"No, thanks, cutie. I'll manage."

He smiled and nearly said something else but I had already turned away, heading quickly to the bank of elevators, where one opened immediately. As the doors were closing, I caught sight of something so disturbing that I immediately tried to punch the door open. Too late, they closed and I was heading up.

A tall man had been moving purposely toward me. A tall man wearing a bow tie.

25.

The elevator doors opened on the third floor.

I half expected to see the same man in the bow tie appear, but, as far as I could tell, I was alone on the third floor. And if anything, the floor appeared even bigger and more spacious than the ground floor. Row after row of endless shelving that stretched as far as the eye could see, all lit gloomily by halogen lighting that dully reflected off the scuffed acrylic flooring.

Cryptic signs with seemingly random words and numbers pointed in various directions, apparently of use to only those who spoke Librarian.

Since I hadn't yet seen a sign that said "Occult Reading Room" and my time was rapidly running out, I decided to try something new in my bag of tricks: remote viewing.

Or, in my case, *nearby* viewing.

I closed my eyes and quieted my mind and thought about what I wanted. The Occult Reading Room. Interestingly, the young kid downstairs came into view...followed immediately by the man in the bow tie. I blinked, refocused, and another image came to mind, swimming up from the black depths like a creature from the deep. Except this was an image of a doorway, and it was to my right and up another hallway.

My consciousness returned quickly; my eyes snapped open.

Whoa.

I hung a right and followed a row of books to the south wall. Once there, I headed north and soon came across the very same doorway I had just seen in my mind's eye.

Unbelievable.

The sign above said "Occult Reading Room," and as I stepped through the open door, I was distinctly aware of the faint sound of an elevator door opening.

26.

The Occult Reading Room was surprisingly bright.

A young man with bright blue eyes and a short beard that came to a point was manning the front desk. He looked up from the pages of an old book that looked like it belonged on the set of a Harry Potter film. I glanced down at the open page and saw various diagrams and words that I was certain were not in English. Then again, I was never very adept at reading upside down.

"I'm looking for information about a man."

He pointed to a card catalog on a nearby wall. "We're still in the process of computerizing the card catalog, but everything we have is in there."

"Sure, um..."

He smiled warmly. "You have no clue how to use a card catalog."

"I haven't used one since high school, and even then I didn't know what I was doing. Mostly I just needed a place to hide my gum."

He shook his head. "You're not chewing any gum now, are you?"

"No."

He grinned. "Then come on."

At the card catalog, he patiently showed me how to search under "subject." I thanked him and he had just returned to his epic tome, when I heard footsteps approaching in the outer hallway.

From my position at the card catalog I had a view of the entrance into the Occult Reading Room. No one was there. Indeed, the footsteps seemed to be receding now, perhaps heading down a side aisle.

I debated following, but remembered the reading room would be closing in just a few minutes.

The creep in the bow tie had me on edge. Had he been the same tall man I had seen in Kingsley's building? I didn't know, but I could count on one hand the number of men I had seen wearing bow ties this last year. Hell, in the last five years.

And now I had seen two in one day.

Coincidence? I think not.

And, yes, I thought back to Fang's words: *"There are no coincidences, Moon Dance."*

Although my sixth sense was always a little sketchy during the day, I wasn't picking up on any danger. Still, I stepped briefly outside and scanned the hallway. No one there.

Back at the card catalog, I found the drawer labeled "Ma-Mi," and started flipping through the ancient cards, my sharp nails and heightened dexterity making it easy to whip through them rapidly.

My blurred fingers stopped on a name that I wasn't entirely prepared to see. In fact, I had already given up the search as a lost cause. But there, on the yellowed piece of paper, were the words: *Archibald Maximus: My Life as a Mystic, Alchemist and Philosopher.*

"Unbelievable," I whispered.

Dazed, I jotted down the Dewey Decimal Numbers and proceeded to hunt through the reading room. The energy in the Occult Reading Room, I noticed, was off. I wasn't sure why, truth be known, but I wondered if it had something to do with the room's darker contents. Indeed, as I read some of the spines of the books, I could see why:

A Compleat History of Magick, Amulets and Superstitions.

Vampires: Alive and Well and Living Among Us.

Magick in Theory and Practice.

Curse Tablets and Binding Spells.

Lycans: Our Wolf Brothers.

Additionally, there were countless books on alchemy, magic, demonology, divination, Satanism, freemasonry, Middle Eastern magical grimoires.

Books on East Asian magical practices, Tibetan secret practices, books on the Tarot and raising the dead. Some of the books looked ancient, so old that I was afraid to touch them. Many of them were surrounded by a darkness visible to my eyes, similar to the darkness that had surrounded my son. Sometimes I heard whispering as I went down the aisles, as if I were not alone.

One book in particular radiated a blackness so dark that I gave it a wide berth. Even still, as I stepped past it, I heard whispering in my ear, "Sister, come to us..."

Sweet Jesus.

Shaking, I finally reached the aisle I wanted. Ignoring the slithering, psychic chattering that now seemed to come from everywhere, I quickly ran my pointed nail along the books' spines, praying like hell that the book I needed would be there.

Not this row. I scanned the next one and the next.

And there it was. I literally breathed a sigh of relief.

I carefully removed the narrow volume. The book was clearly ancient, bound in leather and written in what appeared to be vellum, sheep skin. The title was clear enough and written in modern English, which surprised me since the book was obviously bound centuries earlier.

But I didn't have time to think about it.

The young man behind the desk was now carefully stacking his books. As he turned away from me, I quickly slipped the narrow volume down the front of my jeans.

I made haste, exiting via a different route, ignoring the beseeching cries from some of the darker books. At the desk, the young man smiled and asked if I had found what I was looking for.

I said maybe, smiled, and exited the Occult Reading Room, noting for the first time that the aura around him was violet and utterly beautiful.

On the way out of the library, walking a little funny, I didn't see the man with the bow tie.

27.

I was sitting by my son's side.

The sun was setting and I was feeling excited and nervous and guilty as hell. I thought back to my first few nights as a vampire, and I was certain that I wasn't aware that a drastic change had occurred. Not yet. It would take a few days.

Indeed, I just remember sleeping and healing, and it wasn't until a few days later, at home, that the cravings began. Cravings for the red stuff.

I looked down at my son. In a matter of days or hours or minutes—or perhaps it had already happened, he would go from being a sweet little boy, to an immortal with a hunger for blood and a penchant for turning into a little vampire bat. No doubt, a cute little vampire bat.

And be with you forever.

I heard the words again. And again. And again.

I suddenly had an image of me fighting traffic for an eternity, listening to infomercials for an eternity. An eternity of bad hair days, of showering and putting on deodorant. An eternity of drinking blood.

Mostly, though, an eternity alone.

I never feared death. Death was the natural order of things and I was always certain that there was something waiting for us beyond. If so, then why fear death?

But I would never discover what lay beyond, would I? I would never see the face of God. I would never sit across from Jesus or Buddha or Krishna. Instead, I would only sit across from a TV, or whatever passed for a TV in the far future, while yet another infomercial for yet another magic dishrag.

The medallion had been my answer, of course. It had been my way out of the immortality game. The immortality prison. My chance to escape an eternity of doldrums.

But not anymore.

The sun was setting. I knew this because I could feel some of the weight on my shoulders diminishing. Also, there was a small tingling that was beginning to creep up along my spine. A sort of awakening perhaps. An awakening to all that I could be. I ached for the sun to set. Longed for it to do so.

Hurry, dammit.

Next to me, my son stirred.

"Mommy?"

"Hi baby," I said.

"Mommy, I had a bad dream."

I had no doubt. "I know, honey. I know."

28.

I stayed by my son's side for many hours.

My ex-husband sent me a text, asking how our son was doing. I told him he was improving, and Danny sent a happy face and an "XO." As in hugs and kisses.

I didn't reply. Receiving X's and O's from Danny felt all kinds of weird. We were long, long past the days of X's and O's.

Now we were just "ex's." Period.

My son's illness had somehow brought me closer to Danny—or, more accurately, brought him closer to me. Except, I didn't want him closer. Not anymore. I forgave, but I didn't forget. How could I forget getting banned from my own kids? How could I forget the blackmail and the heartlessness?

How could I forget the blatant cheating?

I couldn't. Not ever.

In fact, I went back into the message and erased his "XO," shuddering as I did so.

Anthony slipped in and out of consciousness. Doctors and nurses came and went, as well, drawing blood, checking his vitals, seemingly impressed by his progress. Everything, that is, except his lowering body temperature.

Anthony described one of his dreams to me, and as he spoke, my heart broke. He described a dark room. In the room was something calling to him, asking him to come closer. He didn't want to get closer. He wanted to turn and run but he was trapped. In fact, there was no door in the room. No door and no light, but something was in there with him, asking him again to come closer. Afraid and crying and screaming my name, he finally turned and faced what was calling to him.

Except he couldn't see it. The voice told him he was a good boy and to step just a little bit closer. He did so. The voice had told him: *good good, that's a good boy, now come closer still.* And he did so. One tentative step at a time, and each time he drew closer to the voice, he was praised. And when he was certain he was standing in front of whatever was calling to him, hands seized him, squeezing him, hurting him, and, while he told me this story, he burst into tears and so did I.

Nurses came running. I assured them that everything was okay. And when we were alone, I hugged my son tight and he lapsed into a deep sleep.

As he slept, I cracked the ancient book open with excitement and trepidation. I had no clue what it contained, and I had waited until this moment to scan the contents. The title had given me hope that the book would be written in English, but a part of me still feared that it was in Latin, Greek or even Hebrew.

Dust sifted down from the cover, catching some of the light from the lamp near my son's bed. Outside the door, two nurses hurried past. Someone was weeping not too far away. The weeping could have been a mother.

There was a title page...in English, thank God. According to the title page the book had been published...this couldn't be right. What the hell was going on? Had Fang set me up? Was this some kind of sick joke?

Hands shaking, I read the copyright date, and unlike most books that gave copyrights years, this one gave an exact date.

Today's date.

I stared at it long and hard.

Surely someone was playing a joke on me, and the only person who knew I was at the library was Fang, and that was impossible since I was privy to most of Fang's thoughts—

There was, of course, another who knew I was in the library.

The tall man with the bow tie. He knew I was

there. Or, at least, had followed me there. Had he planted the book? And then inserted the corresponding card into the card catalog system?

So weird.

There was only one thing left to do...I turned to the first page and started reading.

29.

It was full dark by the time I pulled out of the hospital.

Danny had come by bearing gifts. He brought Anthony a milkshake from McDonald's and me a bottled water. Danny, of course, knew of my dietary restrictions. He was in a good mood and I didn't appreciate the overly familiar hug he gave me. Also, with Anthony's marked improvements, he was being transferred from the intensive care unit to the immediate care unit, where his team of doctors could still keep an eye on him while he continued to recover.

I didn't know much about anything but *immediate care* sounded a whole hell of a lot better than *intensive care.*

By my reckoning, I had only three days to find an answer for Anthony before my son realized what his mommy had done to him. With father and son chumming it up, I gave Anthony a kiss, nodded at a beaming Danny, and left the hospital with my book.

Now driving, I couldn't help but feel so damn alive and strong. So unstoppable. It was all I could do to sit still in the driver's seat. There was so much energy surging through me that I could have burst into flames. I wanted to fly. I wanted to take flight. To where, I didn't know. Just somewhere. Anywhere. I wanted to be free and feel the wind on my face and watch the earth sweep far below me.

Soon, I thought. *Soon...*

***

Twenty minutes later, I was back at Hero's in Fullerton. After all, Fang had directed me to the university library, which had led me to this strange book, and I needed to know what the hell was going on.

The bar was hopping. I spotted Fang working like a madman behind the bar. He seemed to be making two or three drinks at once. He might be a wanted man, but he was also a helluva bartender. I was tempted to march over to him and demand to know what he knew about the book, but now wasn't a good time. I could wait for the crowd to die down or for him to catch his breath. Because he had a lot of explaining to do.

MOON CHILD

He caught my eye through the sea of people, and I think that was a testament more to our psychic connection than dumb luck. I was a small girl, and the chances of him seeing me through the crowd and dim light were slim to none.

And yet there he was, pausing, staring, smiling.

Hello, Moon Dance.

The words appeared in my thoughts as surely as if he had been standing next to me. I nearly jumped and he laughed lightly from across the room.

I didn't mean to startle you, Moon Dance.

Vampires don't get startled. We get even.

He chuckled again. *So what brings you back? Do you have news about your son?*

Yes, and we need to talk.

Can you give me a few minutes? There are a lot of people who need to get drunk tonight.

Inelegantly put.

I do try. Let's talk in a bit, okay?

But we're not talking, we're thinking. We're freaks.

No, you're the freak.

Fine, I thought. *Think at you soon.*

And from across the bar he winked and got back to work. I stepped outside and looked up at the waxing moon. I reached into my jeans pocket and pulled out a stick of sugar-free gum. Recently, I had discovered that I could chew gum without any ill side effects—other than the occasional minor stomachache—and you can damn well better believe I was going to chew all the gum I could.

117

I marveled at the juicy fruit flavor as my taste buds sprang into action.

I could also smoke without any adverse side effects, like pesky lung cancer. I did that often, too, but tonight the gum chewing was enough.

A glance at the moon invariably conjured thoughts of Kingsley Fulcrum and his own freaky condition. Was this really the last I had seen of the big lug? It felt final. It felt empty.

And yet...

I cared for the big oaf. But maybe it was just a classic example of rebound love. He was the first man I had grown close to after the dissolution of my marriage. All my emotions—and maybe even a small amount of love—had been erroneously dumped onto him.

Confusing him and me.

I had just blown the mother of all bubbles when Fang appeared in the doorway. The bubble burst.

"So let's talk," he said. "I only have a few minutes. And you've got gum in your hair."

30.

We were in my minivan as I caught Fang up on my trip to the college, about twice seeing the gaunt man with the bow tie, and about removing the book from the library—

"You mean you stole it?"

"Big picture, Fang."

"Right."

I next told him about the copyright date, and his eyes narrowed in what I took to be disbelief, and so I reached into the glove compartment to show him the book...but it was gone.

I frantically riffled through the overstuffed glove compartment, pulling out a clump of napkins, insurance papers, bills I still needed to pay, some of Anthony's drawings and...nothing.

"It was here, in the glove box. I just put it in here an hour ago." Stunned, I now looked through the backseat and on the floor between Fang's feet. Had someone broken in and stolen just the book? Did I ever even have the book? Was I losing my friggin' mind? "I don't understand what's happening."

"I don't either, Moon Dance. Tell me more about the book."

"You wouldn't believe me if I told you."

"Try me."

I sat back in my seat, completely shaken. Maybe I shouldn't have been so worked up, especially considering the contents of the book. It was, after all, not so much a book, but a personal message to me. And so I told Fang about it, about how the author appeared to be speaking directly to me. About the advice it contained.

"It was all very spiritual stuff," I said. "It seemed to apply to me directly."

Fang was looking at me through narrowed eyes again. Dubiously, as some would call it. "How so?"

I shrugged. "A lot of advice about staying in the 'light,' about not giving into my 'dark nature.' That those who have been granted premature power have a special challenge in keeping that power in check, to use it for good."

"He's talking about you being a vampire?"

"Not in so many words. The book was very vague about what kind of powers, but it seemed to be directed to anyone who had found themselves in my position. But it could have just as easily been written for a—"

"Werewolf."

"Sure. Or anyone else who suddenly finds themselves in a position of power or authority."

"Wild. But why do you think it was written for you?"

"Hard to pinpoint. It just felt directed at me. It gave a lot of advice, too, too much to talk about now in your ten-minute break."

"And it was copyrighted today?"

I nodded. "Fang, you said that a young guy came in and told you about the Occult Reading Room."

"Right."

"Tell me more about him."

"Like I said, he was a young guy. He came in and soon we were talking about Cal State Fullerton's baseball team. They're in the finals again this year—how their program can consistently put together some of the best teams in college—"

"Focus, Fang."

"Yes, right. He finished his beer and mentioned he had to get back to work in the Occult Reading Room at Cal State's library."

"He said it like that? Not, 'I have to get back to work'?"

"Yeah, you're right. At the time, I thought it had been a little specific, but I blew it off because he had my interest."

I knew about Fang's interest in the occult. His

knowledge of the arcane had come in handy more than once.

He went on, "So, he told me more about the collection; in particular, its thoroughness on nearly all esoteric subjects."

"And he wasn't wearing a bow tie?"

Fang smiled. "Hardly. He couldn't have been more than twenty-five."

"Blue eyes and a pointy beard."

"That's him."

I was thinking about that when my cell rang. I fished it off my van's charger. Danny. "I have to take this," I said to Fang.

"No prob," he said, and leaned over and kissed me on the cheek. "I have to scoot anyway. Love ya."

And before I realized what I was saying, I said, "Love ya, too."

When he was gone, I answered the phone, and Danny didn't waste any time getting to the point. "What the fuck did you do to our boy, you goddamned monster?!"

31.

"Calm down, Danny."

"Don't tell me to calm down, you goddamn freak! You changed him, Sam. *You fucking changed him.* That's why he's so cold. That's why his body temperature is dropping."

"And that's why he's alive, Danny."

"Fuck you, Sam. This is too much. This is just too fucking much. Unbelievable. I hate you, Sam. I hate you more than I've ever hated you."

He went on like this for a few more minutes. I tried to speak, but couldn't get a word in edgewise. Finally, when he took a breath, I said, "He was dying, Danny. He was dying. Do you understand? He would be dead now."

"You don't know that. How could you know

that? You didn't give him a chance. He could have pulled through."

"No, he wouldn't have. I saw his death, Danny. I saw it as plain as day."

"Better he dies a human than be a freak like you."

"You don't mean that—"

"Go to hell, you bitch. I will never forgive you for this or forget this, and I am going to make it my life's fucking mission to drag you down to hell where you belong."

He clicked off, no doubt angrily, just as I received another call. It was from a restricted line. Restricted lines often meant one of two things: telemarketers or cops. In this case, it was the cops. In particular, Detective Sherbet.

"Samantha," he said simply.

"Detective."

"We have a situation here at the hospital. I need to see you asap."

"What's wrong? Is it my son?" My voice instantly went from calm to nearly hysterical.

"Your son is fine, Sam. No, this is something else, and we need to see you asap."

32.

I was sitting with Detective Sherbet in the hospital break room, or one of its break rooms, after a very tense ride from Hero's. My frantic mind had imagined every conceivable, horrific scenario, each one worse than the other.

But never had I imagined this.

The hospital was in complete anarchy. Police everywhere. A mother weeping uncontrollably. Nurses frightened. Doctors frightened. Hell, everyone looked frightened. A very grave Sherbet had shut the break room door behind him and sat across from me.

Detective Sherbet and I had become close over these past few months. Not so close that I had disclosed to him my super-secret identity, but pretty damn close. Sherbet, no idiot, was aware that some really freaky shit was going down in his city. He knew I was connected to it, and in fact, might be the freakiest of them all. To his credit, he had yet to confront me about who—or what—I might know. Rather, he'd been approaching this from the outside, nibbling away at the edges. Perhaps his approach was a good one: absorbing small details at a time.

Sherbet was a big man, but not as big as Kingsley or my new detective friend out of Huntington Beach. If anything, he looked like a panda bear: salt-and-pepper hair, way too round around the middle, serious yet playful. And, if necessary, tough as hell.

"We have a child missing," he said simply. We were sitting at a round and heavily scarred table. His belly, I noted, actually rested on the edge of the table.

My own stomach sank. "What do you mean?"

"A patient, a child, was kidnapped not too long ago by an unknown male."

My heart froze. "When?"

"Just over thirty minutes ago. Kidnapped here, from the hospital."

"Oh my God."

"The hospital is on lockdown. No one in or out. Absolute insanity." As he spoke, Sherbet was watching me closely. The muscles along his hairy forearms moved just under his thin skin, as he clenched and unclenched his fists. "The city of

Orange isn't my beat, but the guys here are good friends of mine. When a child goes missing all available hands come running. When I first heard the report, I thought of your son here."

"But he's okay." I knew this because I had already checked on him.

He nodded. "Sam, the boy was kidnapped from your son's old room."

"I don't understand."

"Your son, from what I understand, was recently moved from ICU to immediate care." I wasn't following but he continued on. "Another boy took your son's room. Within thirty minutes, he was gone."

"Oh, my God."

Through the closed doors, I could hear someone barking an order. A child was crying somewhere. In fact, many children were crying.

Sweet Jesus. What was going on?

Sherbet went on, "The parents were down in the cafeteria getting some coffee and preparing for another all-nighter when they got the news."

"Were there any witnesses?" My voice sounded hollow and distant.

"Oh, yeah. A man comes in claiming to be an uncle. Charming, smooth as hell, apparently. Says everything right. Front desk lets the bastard right in. Same with the nurses up here. Against protocol left and right. Heads will roll. Yet these same people don't remember letting the guy in. I don't understand any of it."

"They don't remember letting him, but they let him in?"

"Something like that."

"As in no memory of doing it?"

"Right." Sherbet frowned at me. The muscles of his forearm continued to undulate.

"What happened next?"

"You'll never believe it."

"Try me," I said.

"Better I show you."

He led me out of the break room and over to the room I was so familiar with, the same room my son had occupied for the past few days. Except now there was something vastly different about the room.

The entire window was missing.

33.

Sherbet said, "A minute or two after stepping into the room, the nurses heard what sounded like an explosion. When they rushed in to investigate, the boy was gone and the window was broken."

I was speechless. Beyond speechless. I couldn't formulate words. All I wanted to do was run to my son again and check on him, to hold him close and protect him forever.

What the hell was happening?

"For the love of God, Sam, what's going on?"

"I don't know, Detective, I swear—" I stopped when a disturbing image came to mind. "What did the man look like?"

"Tall. Caucasian. Dressed in slacks and a blazer. A blue blazer—Sam, what's wrong?"

"Just go on," I said. I had braced myself against the wall. Although I had little use for my lungs, they suddenly felt constricted, as if an anaconda had curled around my chest and was squeezing, squeezing. "Was he wearing anything else?"

Detective Sherbet was watching me closely.

"A bow tie," he said.

"Oh, shit."

"What do you know, Sam? Dammit, what the hell's going on here?"

"He was following me today."

"Who was following you today?"

"The man with the bow tie."

Sherbet blinked. "If he was following you, then why in the devil would he kidnap the boy?"

"The man was after Anthony, I think."

"Sweet Jesus, Sam."

"And got the wrong boy. He was just a few minutes too late."

"Why would he want your son?"

"He's trying to get to me."

"Who's trying to get to you?"

"I don't know."

"Who is he?"

"I don't know."

"Why does he want you?"

That I did know. Or, at least, I suspected I knew. "I have something he wants."

"Who is he, Sam? And dammit, don't tell me you don't know. You know something. I can feel it. You're holding back and now is not the time to hold back. There's a sick little boy out there who needs immediate medical attention, who's terrified and possibly hurt."

Sherbet had a son of his own, about the same age as Anthony, in fact. I thought about how Sherbet had been such a good friend to me. I also thought about how he was so close to the truth. To my secret. I looked into his eyes now. His desperate and wild eyes. I thought about the little missing boy —a missing boy that was supposed to have been Anthony. My heart broke for him and his family, and I realized that my secret could be a secret no more. At least not with Detective Sherbet.

"Can we talk somewhere more private?"

"No, Sam. We talk here."

"Please, Detective."

He didn't like it. "Fine," he said. "We'll talk in my squad car."

34.

His squad car was an unmarked Ford Crown Victoria, and he was parked in a handicapped spot directly in front of the hospital. The car was immaculate, as I suspected it would be. Not even a wadded-up bag of donuts, which I half expected to find.

As he slid in, he clicked the doors locked. "It's just me and you, kiddo," he said. "Now talk."

"I have an artifact," I started. "A very valuable artifact for some people. I suspect that whoever took the boy wants this artifact. No doubt he thought he was taking my son."

"Ransom," said Sherbet. He hadn't taken his eyes off me.

"That's what I'm thinking."

"And the man in the bow tie?"

"I have no idea who he is."

"But he was following you?"

I nodded. "Yeah, I think so."

Sherbet absorbed these strange details silently, his fine investigative mind sorting them out mentally, labeling them and filing them in his mental file folders. "What's the artifact, Samantha?"

Sherbet was staring at me. I could hear his heart beating steadily, strongly. Sherbet smelled of aftershave and potatoes.

I took a deep breath, held it, and looked my friend in the eye. Sherbet returned my stare, his eyes wide and hungry, searching for information.

"Please, Samantha," he said. "Talk to me."

I continued staring at him, and finally came to a decision. I said, "I'm not what you think I am, Detective."

"What the devil does that mean, Sam?"

"When I was attacked six years ago, I was changed forever."

"No shit, Sam. An attack like that would change any—"

"That's not what I meant, Detective. It changed me in a physical sense. In an eternal sense, too."

"Eternal? What the devil are you talking—wait. Good God, you're not telling you're one of those were-thingies?"

I smiled despite the seriousness of the situation. "No, Detective. I'm a vampire."

35.

"A vampire?" he said.

"Yes."

"And you're serious?"

"As a corpse."

"I don't know whether to laugh or be afraid."

"You can laugh, if you want. Lord knows I've done it a few times. Of course, my laughter usually turns into tears. But you certainly don't need to be afraid, Detective."

Yet another police car pulled up to the hospital. A young officer dashed out and headed for the hospital's main doors. Through it all, Sherbet hadn't taken his eyes off me. I didn't blame him.

"I have a secret, too," he said finally.

"Oh no," I said. "Please don't tell me you're the

Werewolf King or something."

He chuckled lightly. "No, but I would have loved to see the look on your face."

"What's your secret, Detective? Seems like a good night to spill them."

"I've known you were a vampire for some time."

"Really?"

"It's the only thing that made sense. Your strange disease, the dead gang banger drained of blood, the punch through the bulletproof glass, the dead prisoner."

"Why didn't you say anything?"

"Because it was a new theory and I was still debating whether or not I was going insane."

"A question I've asked myself a thousand times."

"I have another secret," he confessed.

"I don't think I can handle any more secrets," I said.

"I've seen *Twilight* five times."

I wasn't sure I'd heard him right. "You saw *what* five times?"

"*Twilight*. My boy loves it. He can't get enough of it. We've seen the sequels a few times, too. Also, I watched them for, you know, research."

Detective Sherbet loved his boy. Of that there was no doubt. That he had been worried sick that his young son was showing early signs of homosexuality was almost comical. With that said, I had been touched by Sherbet's ability to come to terms with the concept. If anything, he loved his boy even more. Still, the thought of the gruff detective sitting through the various naked torso scenes in *Twilight* and its sequels for "research" would normally have had me laughing so hard that I might have peed. But not tonight.

"Anyway," he said, clearly embarrassed. "You could say I'm something of a vampire expert now."

"I see," I said, and now I did laugh. "I hadn't realized I was sitting next to an expert."

He laughed, too, but then quickly turned somber. "But those are just movies. This is real, isn't it, Sam?"

"I'm afraid so."

"You really are a vampire."

I shrugged, my old defense kicking in. "I don't know what I am, Detective."

"What does that mean?"

"It means I'm the same person I've always been, except sometimes when I'm not. It means that I feel the same that I've always felt, except sometimes when I don't. It means I act the same, think the same, and do the same things I've always done.

"Except when you don't," said Sherbet.

"Yes, exactly. It means I'm still me. I'm still a mom. I'm still a woman. I'm still a sister. And I'm still a friend."

"But you're also something else. Something more."

I nodded. "And sometimes I'm that, too."

We were silent for a minute or two. The detective's heart rate, I noted, had increased significantly. "It happened six years ago, didn't it?"

I nodded.

"It left you...the way you are now."

"Yes."

"You never asked for this, did you?"

I shook my head.

"And it's ripped your life apart, hasn't it?"

I nodded and fought the tears. Enough crying. I was sick of crying, but it felt so damn nice to be understood, especially by a man I respected and admired so much.

"And now you're doing all you can to keep it together."

Shit. The tears started. Damn Detective Sherbet.

He reached over and patted my hand. A grandfatherly gesture. A warm gesture.

"So you believe me?" I asked.

"I believe something. What that is, I don't know. Most of me thinks you're insane, or that I'm insane. Most people would think, in the least, that you're a hazard to your kids."

"Do you think I'm a hazard to my kids?"

"No. I think you're a wonderful mother. I really believe that."

"Thank you," I said, moved all over again.

Sherbet touched the back of my hand again. My instinct was, of course, to retract my hand, but I didn't. Not this time. His fingertips explored my skin, almost like a blind man would the face of his lover. "Your cold skin always confused me. And your skin disease never felt right."

"Because it wasn't."

He nodded. "And Ira Lang...sweet Jesus. The visiting room."

Sherbet was referring to the time a month or so ago when I had punched through a bullet-proof piece of glass to grab a piece of shit named Ira Lang, and proceeded to let him know what I thought of him threatening me and my kids.

"You killed him, Sam."

I said nothing. I wasn't admitting anything, especially to a homicide investigator.

"You nearly ripped his head off."

I kept saying nothing.

"Of course, I should arrest you. For his murder, and for anyone else who's gone missing or been killed on any of your other cases." He turned his shoulder and propped a meaty elbow up on the seat's head rest. "Just tell me one thing, Sam: do you kill people for blood?"

"No."

"Do you drink blood?"

His tone was challenging. I felt like a daughter confronted by her father about smoking weed or drinking booze.

"I have to," I said, looking away.

He stared at me so long and hard that I wanted to crawl under a rock.

"Please don't judge me," I finally said. "I never asked for this."

"I'm not judging, Sam. I'm just trying to wrap my brain around all of this. I mean, a part of me suspected something was up, and perhaps even a very small part of me began to believe...this. But to hear it now, from a pretty young investigator I've grown to admire, is something else entirely."

"I'll deny everything, Detective. So let's get that clear now."

I wasn't looking at him but I felt him grin. I sensed only confusion and compassion and more confusion from him. And also a steady sense of alarm. But not for his own health or well-being. We still had a missing boy out there, after all.

"And I'll never admit to watching the *Twilight* movies," he said.

"I'll take your secret to my grave," I said.

"I thought vampires were immortal," he said.

"We'll see."

"So what do we do about Eddy?" said Sherbet. "The kidnapped boy?"

"If it's a ransom," I said. "Then I'll be hearing from his abductor."

Sherbet nodded. "Makes sense. And his abductor...would he also be a vampire?"

"More than likely," I said.

"And what's this about a relic?"

I reached inside my jeans pocket and removed the medallion. I didn't trust it anywhere except on my person. He turned on the car's interior light, and I showed him the golden disc.

"It's a necklace with ruby roses," he said.

"Your observational skills are second to none, Detective."

"Don't sass me, young lady. What's so special about this?"

"It's reputed to reverse vampirism."

"Ah," he said. "And that's a good thing?"

"For some."

"And you don't want to give it up?"

"I can't," I said. "Under any circumstances."

"Even to save a little boy?"

I put the medallion back in my pocket. Just having it out made me nervous.

"I need it," I said.

He heard the anguish in my voice, and since Sherbet also happened to be a helluva detective, he looked at me sharply. "Your son," he said.

I buried my face in my hands.

"You need it to change your son back, don't you?"

Now I was rocking in my seat and crying, and talking incomprehensibly about saving my son, and doing all I had to do to keep him from dying, and knowing I was a horrible mother, but what else could I do? I loved him so much, and I had a chance to save him, and I had to take it, I had to take it...

And as I babbled nearly incoherently, Detective Sherbet reached out and put his arm around my shoulders and pulled me in close and told me that everything was going to be okay. Somehow, someway, everything was going to be okay...

36.

Mary Lou arrived an hour or so later with Tammy.

They had stopped at McDonald's and had sneaked in a Big Mac for Anthony. I told them Anthony was probably too weak to eat, but boy was I wrong. He devoured the sandwich in a few quick bites and was looking for more. He next pounded his sister's fries, and I waited for what I was sure was coming next:

Upchuck city.

Food, for me, lasts only a few minutes before it comes up violently. But Anthony never did vomit. Instead, he complained slightly of an upset stomach and I realized what was happening. Although only a half inch or so above his skin, his aura was still there. His humanity was still there. For now. Until the change overcame him completely. By contrast, his sister, who was sitting on the edge of his bed and playing "Angry Birds" on my sister's cell phone, shone like a beacon in the night. Pale yellows and reds, streaked with silvers and golds, surrounded her body many feet or more, sometimes flaring like mini-nuclear explosions on the surface of the sun.

But not Anthony. His aura was only a fine dusting of light. Almost an afterthought.

Shit.

His last meal, I thought. *Or close to it.*

I was, admittedly, torn. I knew I had to find Archibald Maximus asap, especially since his book had given me an intriguing clue. From what I gathered, he lived in the mountains above San Bernardino, Lake Arrowhead or Big Bear, one of those, both popular ski resorts. With Anthony getting better, and simultaneously losing his mortality, now was as good a time as any to set out for the mountains and Mr. Maximus.

But the missing boy was tearing me to pieces. An innocent family had gotten caught up in my insanity, and now their boy was missing, having been abducted by a true monster.

Who was Bow Tie? A vampire? I had no doubt, unless the medallion could reverse other supernatural curses, which it very well might. That he jumped from a third-floor hospital room, leaving behind no evidence—it turns out he had thrown a chair through the window—could mean anything. I suspected someone like Kingsley could withstand such a fall. After all, I had seen him in his wolf's form leap nine stories without missing a beat. Whether or not Kingsley could perform such an act in his human form, I didn't know. There was so much I didn't know.

There was a family not very far from this room who had been torn to pieces. All because of my actions. I had to do something.

I looked again at the faint aura around my son's body. I still had time. Not much, granted, but at least a day and a half, maybe two.

I stood and paced and my daughter ignored me. That her little brother was suddenly doing much better didn't seem to matter much to her. The faith of children. No doubt she always assumed he would get better.

My sister was watching me with huge eyes. She alternately looked at Anthony and I saw her confusion. She suspected something, too. But not enough to confront me about it, and I couldn't talk to her about it, not now, and not in present company. She was just going to have to keep wondering.

Where would the bastard have gone? Would he be contacting me soon? Had he realized his mistake and simply killed the boy? Would he next be coming after Anthony?

I didn't know, but I didn't have long to wait.

After pacing a few more minutes and wondering

also what Danny was up to, my cell phone rang. Another restricted number.

I answered with a simple hello.

"Miss Moon," said a man with a heavy French accent. "I believe you have something I want."

37.

I stepped out of the room and into the hallway.

"Who is this?"

"Never mind that, Samantha Moon of the Moon Agency. I realize I have made a critical error, but perhaps not all is lost."

He paused and I could have jumped in with another wasted question. Instead, I waited, breathless, realizing without a doubt that a vampire was on the other end of the line.

He spoke again in his heavy French accent. "The real question here, Samantha Moon, is how much compassion you have for your fellow man. Or, in this case, boy."

"Go on," I said.

"Give me the medallion and I give you the boy,

alive."

"You're a piece of shit."

"A desperate piece of shit, Samantha Moon. I know what you are, and I know that you know what I am. At least now you do. Who else would want the medallion?" He paused as my mind reeled. He went on: "And perhaps you don't realize that the longer you live, the harder you are to kill. Has this occurred to you?"

"Fuck you."

"I see it hasn't. Well, let me assure you, I am old. Very, very old. And I am desperate to end this existence, Miss Moon. Desperate. I am tired of living, and I cannot die. Not by silver. Not by anything. Do you understand me?"

I said nothing. Thinking was hard. The man's voice was so damn...hypnotic. Even for me. I could see why anyone and everyone would have given him what he wanted. It took all my effort to keep my thoughts clear. I felt him pushing in, even from a distance, trying to claim my thoughts.

"Ah, I see you are not new at this, Miss Moon. Not everyone, undead included, can resist me. Very well. Let me assure you that I am tired of living, and I will bring this entire fucking planet to hell with me, if I have to. The boy means nothing to me. Your son means nothing to me. You mean nothing to me. Nothing has any meaning except my own death, my removal from this earth. Do you understand me?"

"Yes," I said, aware that I was indeed speaking

on my own free will.

"Nothing can end my life except for one thing, and one thing alone. The medallion. The wonderfully enchanted medallion that I have searched so long for. So very, very long."

"Where are you?"

"I am not far, my dear."

"How do I find you?"

For an answer, I suddenly had an image of a rooftop. But this wasn't just any rooftop. There were stairs leading everywhere. The roof itself had many levels and platforms and turrets. It was the roof to the Mission Inn in Riverside. I would know it anywhere.

"Good, good. You recognize this. Do not speak of it, my dear, or I will kill this little one and fetch another and another and another until you bring to me what I want. Do you understand?"

I thought of my son. I thought of many, many things, all of which I shielded from the bastard who kept probing my thoughts. "I do."

"Then I will see you in two hours."

And the line went dead.

38.

I found Sherbet inside the office of the hospital's public relations administrator. Through the open door, I saw a young couple sitting together. The couple had their backs to me and appeared to be listening to someone in command. No doubt the captain of Orange Police Department's Investigative Division. The woman mostly had her face buried in her hands, while her husband had his arms around her, comforting her. I couldn't see their faces.

Sherbet saw me and stepped outside. He read my expression instantly. The man was damn good.

"Our guy called," he said.

"Yes."

"Where is he?"

I shook my head. "I have to do this alone or he kills the boy."

"No way, Sam. I'm going with you, along with some of my boys."

I shook my head. "He will know, Detective. He'll know and he'll kill the boy."

"How will he know?"

"In ways you won't understand."

He didn't like it. "Maybe he's bluffing."

"He's not."

"How do you know?"

"Call it a hunch."

"Not good enough, Sam."

"Fine," I said. "Because he's a very, very old vampire who cares little for anything, if at all. He will kill the boy and find another."

"We'll catch him."

"And risk the boy's life?"

Sherbet looked away, so frustrated that he growled. He rubbed his bristled face repeatedly. "I don't like it, Sam."

"Who would?"

"So what are you going to do?"

"I'm going to get the boy."

"How?"

"Any way I can."

"Are you going to hand over the medallion?"

"I don't know."

"If you give up the medallion, what happens to your son?"

"I don't want to think about it," I said.

He continued rubbing his face. Nervous energy crackled through him. "I don't like it, Sam," he said again.

"Neither do I," I said and turned to leave. "I gotta go."

"Sam," he called after me.

I stopped and looked back. The big detective looked sick with worry. "Please be careful, kid."

"I wouldn't have it any other way."

And I turned and left.

39.

I was tempted to call Fang, but I didn't.

Like the detective, he would want to come, too. Unlike the detective, he didn't know what the hell he was doing, and the last I checked, Fang didn't even have a weapon.

Which was probably a moot point anyway, since according to the vampire, nothing could kill him, silver included. *"And I am desperate to end this existence, Miss Moon. Desperate. I am tired of living, and I cannot die. Not by silver. Not by anything."*

Sweet Jesus.

Of course, that's if he was telling me the truth.

I merged onto the 57 North, slipping into the fast lane, and gave the minivan a lot of gas. I loved my little minivan. Sure, it screamed soccer mom, but it was so handy and smooth and comfortable that I just didn't give a shit what people thought.

Traffic was light and fast, which is the way I liked it. Brake lights, blinker lights, headlights and street lights all mostly blended together with the zigzagging streaks of energy that filled my vision, the glowing filaments that made it possible for me to see into the night.

I gave the van more gas and thought about the medallion. I wasn't sure what I was going to do. Whoever Bow Tie was, he surely wasn't going to accept anything less than the medallion.

One problem: As noted by Detective Sherbet, I needed it to give my son back his mortality.

My phone rang. Another restricted call. At this point, it could have been anyone, from a vampire kidnapper to Sherbet. It was neither.

"Hey, Sunshine," said Chad Helling, my ex-partner, a man who did not know my super-secret identity...only that I had a rare skin disease.

"Hey, Romeo."

"I heard about the shitty business at the hospital. Is your son okay?"

"My son's fine, which is more than I can say for another little boy."

"You need me to come down?" he asked. "Once a partner, always a partner."

"Thanks, Chad, but I'll manage."

"I know you will. You always do." He paused. "You have news about Archibald Maximus."

"Yes, how did you—never mind. You could always read my mind."

I grinned to myself. He was right, and there was nothing psychic about it. I said, "Once a partner, always a partner."

He chuckled. "Anyway, no luck with Mr. Archibald Maximus, although something strange did turn up."

"How strange?"

"Oh, it's nothing. Never mind."

"Tell me, dammit."

"Easy, girl. Okay, fine. There was an Archibald Maximus who died fifty years ago."

I did find that interesting, but Chad didn't need to know that. "And this helps me how?"

"Well, the strange part is that his family and friends reported seeing him on two other occasions."

"After his death?"

"Right."

"And how do you know this?"

"The wife filed a report. She wanted his body exhumed."

"Did they?"

"No."

I chewed on this. But Chad didn't need to know I was chewing on this. Instead, I said, "Well, thanks for wasting the last three minutes of my life."

"Anytime. Be safe, Sunshine."

"Jerk."

And he clicked off, laughing.

***

The 57 North merged into the 91 East. I was soon shooting past the 80 mph mark—and still there were drivers riding my ass. You can never go fast enough in southern California.

I was cruising at 85 mph and had just settled in for the hour-long drive to Riverside when my cell phone chirped. A text message. I rummaged through my purse, swerving slightly into the next lane, until I found the iPhone. A text from Fang.

Something's wrong, he wrote. *I can feel it. What's going on? Where are you going?*

Jesus, our connection was growing stronger. I wasn't sure how I felt about that, but maybe there was something greater at work here than I thought. Maybe Fang was destined to be something more. Much more. I didn't know, but I certainly couldn't think about it now.

I rapidly typed out my reply: *Just getting ice cream with Tammy. On our way to Cold Stone now.*

Bullshit, Sam. Why do I feel a tremendous sense of...dread.

Maybe you had some bad Chinese.

A car horn blasted next to me, and I straightened out my minivan. Apparently I had given the guy next to me a fright. I waved an apology and he waved back with his middle finger.

Enough with the bad Chinese, Sam. Please. What's going on? I'm worried sick over here.

It's better if you don't know, Fang. I'm sorry.

Let me help you. Please. I've never felt this way before.

Welcome to my world, I thought. Instead, I wrote: *I'm sorry, Fang. I'll call later. Love you.*

Love you? Now what the hell had gotten into me?

40.

The Mission Inn is a national treasure.

And it's found right here in downtown Riverside, a city that isn't much of a national treasure. For me, Riverside conjures images of heat and gangs and neighborhoods that aren't so nice. A false image, surely, as its downtown is actually quite nice, and boasts some cool bars and nice restaurants. But, most importantly, it boasts the Mission Inn, getaway to presidents and celebrities alike, where thousands have been married and many tens of thousands have passed through.

After negotiating through some heavy downtown traffic, in which I passed exactly three prostitutes and a guy dressed like Lady Gaga, and parked in a small parking lot across the street from the inn. There I sat quietly, closed my eyes, and tried to get a feel for the place. Eyes closed, I sensed lots of movement, lots of happy people, lots of great moments. The Mission Inn is a special place.

I next tried to get a sense of any danger, of what I might be up against, but the place was just too big for me to get a feel for it. Either that, or my thoughts were too scattered to focus correctly. Then again, I still didn't entirely know what I was doing.

Next I focused on the roof, rising as surely as if I was physically floating above the edifice. The suites up here were nicer, more expensive. The roof area, which sported many walkways and ramps that led to various floors and balconies, looked like something out of a medieval fairy tale. A handful of couples were sitting together on their balconies, enjoying the night, smoking, drinking, kissing, writhing.

Uh oh.

Above it all was one of the inn's three majestic domes, this one a mosaic jewel that crowned this section of the inn, and as it came into view in my mind, I gasped.

There was a darkness within. It surrounded the dome as surely as the dark halo had surrounded my son. I tried to dip into the dome, but I couldn't. Somehow, I was blocked. More, I didn't *want* to go inside. The dome repelled me, horrified me.

He's in there, I thought.

And that's when my cell phone rang. Restricted

J.R. RAIN

call, of course. It was him, I knew it. How an ancient vampire knew how to restrict his calls, I hadn't a clue.

I clicked on and he spoke immediately: "You're here," he said. "I can feel another."

"What does that mean?"

"It means I can feel another of our kind, Miss Moon."

"I'm nothing like you."

He laughed sharply, so sharply that my ear hurt. "Oh, we are very much alike, my dear."

"You're in the dome," I said.

"Yes," he said, and sounded impressed. "With the other bats."

"Is the boy with you?"

"You mean that sickly little thing? Sure, he's here somewhere, but he's not long for this world. I should probably just help him along."

"You touch him, and you'll never get the medallion."

"Oh, relax, my dear. I won't touch him...yet. I'll see if you'll play by my rules first. If so, he may be spared. If not, there's going to be blood tonight."

"Enough with the threats, asshole. I have the medallion."

He veritably hissed with pleasure. "Good, good! Then I expect to see you soon," and he clicked off.

41.

The massive hotel stretched from city block to city block, surrounded by a low, medieval-style brick wall.

An array of lights lit the hotel, and the building's sheer complexity of style was enough to nearly overwhelm the senses, everything from Spanish Gothic, Mission Revival, Moorish Revival, Renaissance Revival and Mediterranean Revival. I know something about architecture. If I hadn't been an investigator, I would have been an architect. And the inn was a wonder to behold.

I was in a parking lot on Orange Street, along the south east side of the building. There was a side opening here that I was familiar with, one that led to a small bar that Danny and I had frequented many times, where we drank wine and beer and ate lightly breaded chicken strips and listened to a talented cellist and talked about our days.

Those days were long gone.

Years ago, before I met Danny, my first visit to the hotel had been a laughable one. I was running late to my then-boyfriend's cousin's wedding. I was in college and working two jobs and I had barely gotten off in time to rush out from Orange County on a Saturday evening. Running in high heels and clutching my dress, I dashed into the first chapel I saw. The wedding was about to start. Feeling self-conscious, I sat in the back row and looked wildly for my boyfriend, assuming he was sitting somewhere in the front. I felt like shit that I had come so late that I couldn't find him, but at least I made it, right? I had never met his cousins, and I didn't know anyone in his family, and so I sat in the back alone, going through the motions of a very Catholic wedding, kneeling and crossing and saying prayers with everyone else.

After the longish wedding, when everyone poured out into the courtyard, I was caught up by a group of women who forced me up a spiraled staircase for pictures. As I continued to scan the milling crowd below for my boyfriend, I paused every so often for the photographer. We took a God-awful amount of pictures, and when I was finally released, I happened to see another chapel on the far side of the courtyard. Another wedding had taken place, and was just now finishing.

And there, exiting through the doors, was my boyfriend.

Exactly. I had gone to the wrong wedding. That's me, Samantha Moon, the original wedding crasher. To this day, I'm certain the bride is wondering who that cute, dark-haired girl was in all her photos.

Back when I could take photos, of course.

Needless to say, that night only went from bad to worse, and my boyfriend and I broke up in an epic fight. I met Danny shortly thereafter and the rest, as they say, is history.

Good times, I thought, as I stepped across the street and headed under the veranda and into the gloomy bar where the cello player had long since disappeared. Now, no one played, and that was a damn shame.

I moved through the lobby and front desks, and through what appeared to be yet another lobby lined with presidential portraits. I assumed these were all the presidents who had stayed here. The hotel felt damn old and I sensed many, many lingering spirits. Hell, if I was a spirit, I would linger here, too. A ghost could do worse than haunt the Mission Inn.

Now with the hair on my neck standing on end, I turned and saw where one spirit was semi-manifesting. Staticy energy formed into the shape of what appeared to be a teenage boy. He was watching me casually from one of the spiraling staircases that led up to the more expensive suites. As I watched him, he took on more shape and made a partial appearance, the crackling energy briefly replaced by a wispy cloud of ectoplasm. Had someone chosen now to take a picture of the staircase, they would have captured an honest-to-God ghost. Anyway, his eyes widened with some surprise when he no doubt realized that I was watching him in return. He came to life, so to speak, and drifted immediately over to me, where he stood in front of me, smiling. Was that a wink?

I could be wrong, but I think he was flirting with me.

Next, the strong impression of a name appeared in my thoughts. "Your name is...Leland?" I asked.

He nodded vigorously, and now other spirits seemed to take note. They were manifesting around us rapidly, like human-shaped sparklers. Some fully formed, although most crackled and spat crackling energy, only vaguely humanoid. Most were dressed in older-style clothing. Some of the men even wore hats.

"Now look what you started, Leland," I whispered to the teen boy.

He frowned, and then shooed the other spirits away, moving quickly to each. The others departed, some clearly irritated, others fading into nothing or zipping away like blazing comets through the hotel. As they did so, I caught a very real little girl watching us from across the room. She was standing next to her mother, her index finger hooked into her mouth. Her wide eyes followed some of the fleeing spirits. Kids can see far more than we realize.

The teen ghost faded in and out of clarity, sometimes reverting to nothing more than a crackling human torch, and other times to a dapper young man who could have hailed from the 1920s. Once, he even made a gesture to dance, holding out his hand as one would lead a woman to the dance floor, and only then did I notice the ambient music playing over the hotel's speakers. A sort of jazzy/classical rag-time, of the type my grandmother would listen to. Had the classical music drawn him downstairs, I wondered, reminding him of his days when he was alive?

I was about to say goodbye and turn away when I noticed something about his face. There was something that looked like blood coating his lower jaw and staining the front of his shirt. I next had the strong hit of a single word: *tuberculosis*.

So Leland had died here at the hotel, long ago, and has been hanging around ever since, his chin and shirt forever stained with the ghostly hint of perhaps his last coughing fit.

"I have to go," I whispered to him, "but thank you for the offer to dance."

As I turned to leave, I realized I had no clue how to actually get up to the dome. I turned back to the young man, and somehow, someway, he was able to read my thoughts, because he was nodding excitedly and motioning for me to follow him. He held out his hand and, feeling rather silly, I reached out and took it—or simulated taking it—knowing full well I looked silly as hell to just about everyone else. Everyone, that is, but the little girl.

He led me quickly through the massive hotel.

42.

We went through some doors—well, he went through them, I had to open them—and once in the outside courtyard, moved quickly past an elegant restaurant that I had always wanted to try. Back in the day, Danny and I were too poor to dine elegantly. Drinks and chicken tenders were about all we could afford.

Anyway, the teen boy led me along the main artery that led down the center of the hotel, past beautiful planters and water fountains and the pool. We plunged under Mediterranean Revival-style archways lit with hanging lanterns, and dashed quickly over Spanish tile that looked both ancient and impenetrable. We passed couples holding hands or sitting contentedly on ornate benches. We passed more crackling spirits, all of which seemed to have somewhere to go.

Now above us, shining like a mother ship descending from the heavens, was the jaw-droppingly beautiful north tower dome. I only had a glimpse of it before the ghost teen disappeared through a closed door. A closed *locked* door.

A very bloody and sheepish face appeared a moment later in the center of the door. Leland smiled and the ancient blood on his lower jaw almost seemed to sparkle.

"Through here?" I asked.

He nodded vigorously. I tried the handle. Locked.

"I don't suppose you can unlock it from the inside, could you?"

He nodded again and disappeared back through the door. I next heard some very odd, lightly scraping sounds from the other side, and shortly his gruesomely handsome face reappeared. He shook his head sadly.

I looked from side to side, and didn't see anyone paying particular attention to us. I then took hold of the doorknob and applied a smidgen of pressure.

The lock shattered and the handle broke off in my hand. Pieces of metal fell everywhere, inside and outside the door.

Lord, I'm a freak.

The shattering lock would surely have attracted some attention, and so I ignored the stares and pushed the door open like I belonged there. I kicked

166

the broken knob inside.

Leland took my hand again, which felt a bit like plunging my hand in a picnic cooler, and led me up a very narrow spiral staircase that was clearly not meant for hotel guests, judging by how rickety and unstable it was. Who used this staircase and why, I didn't know, but it felt unsafe as hell.

I heard the sounds of pots and pans banging, the sizzle of something or other, and someone shouting an order in Spanish. We were behind the kitchen, perhaps in a forgotten storage room, along a forgotten staircase. I suspected this old hotel, with its many additions, had many such forgotten rooms and staircases.

Sometimes our hands broke contact, but the teen boy would always reach back for me. Sometimes I could see the concern on his face, but mostly I saw his excitement. And with each step we took, my inner warning system sounded louder and louder. Perhaps the loudest I had ever heard it sound. So loud now that even the ghost boy turned and looked at me.

Jesus, had he heard my own alarm system?

There was just so much to learn about the spirit world, a world that had unexpectedly opened up to me these past few months.

Now we were at another door. This was unlocked and soon we were standing in a very long and creepy hallway. The hallway had been used for storage. Now, I suspected, it was long since forgotten. Old sinks and clawed bathtubs and disgusting toilets that turned my stomach.

He led me deeper. I noted Leland didn't kick up any dust, whereas I left behind great swirling plumes of the stuff.

We hung a right and soon came upon another narrow flight of wrought-iron stairs. The boy floated up them effortlessly, whereas, I climbed up them as quietly as possible. I felt for the medallion in my pocket, suddenly wishing I had left it in the van, after all.

Lord, if I lost this...

The few breaths I took echoed loudly around me, filling the small space. The ladder seemed like it might creak, but mercifully, it didn't. I followed the boy up, sometimes looking through a pair of ghostly buns.

We reached the upper landing and stood before another door and I had a sense that we were very high up. As high as the mosaic dome, no doubt.

"In here?" I asked.

Leland nodded. He had now made a full appearance, and I could see all the fine details of his handsome young face, a face that was now creased with concern.

Who knew ghosts could crease?

When I reached for the door knob, he seized my wrist with hands solid enough to pull my own away. Crazy goose bumps appeared instantly up and down my arm. He shook his head vigorously.

"It'll be okay," I said quietly. "Thank you for your help."

"Please," Leland said, speaking for the first time, his voice a grating whisper. "There's a very bad man inside."

I smiled and reached out and touched his face. A shiver went through me again.

"I'm pretty bad myself," I said, and opened the door.

43.

The door opened loudly enough to wake the dead.

Hell, maybe it did.

Although I doubted I would ever sneak up on the vampire, any hope of doing that went out the window.

Or through the squeaky door.

The ghost teen stayed behind, clearly worried, and anything that worried a ghost should seriously worry me, too, I figured.

Except, I rarely backed down from a fight, even back in the days when I was very mortal. Bullies and assholes never scared me, and this French vampire piece-of-a-bitch was clearly both.

A narrow catwalk encircled the entire area,

branching off in both directions. Above me was the inverted arch, sealing off the night sky. A small pinprick of moonlight made its way through a window. An open window, actually, and I suddenly realized how the vampire had been coming and going.

Below, the floor dropped down about twenty feet, to what appeared to be more storage. With the dome arching two stories above, there was, in total, about forty to fifty feet of open space here. Big enough for one's voice to echo, and certainly big enough for a giant vampire bat to take flight.

As my eyes fully accustomed to the big, open space, I heard the sound of breathing. Short, frightened gasps. Coming from seemingly everywhere at once.

There, on the far side of the catwalk. A small figure was curled in the fetal position, shivering violently. He was still wearing his thin hospital gown, which was next to useless. Fury raged through me. The boy needed immediate medical attention. The heartless piece of shit. I couldn't imagine the horror this little one had endured.

The catwalk was even more wobbly than the last staircase. As I stepped onto it, the boy's head rolled in my direction. My instincts were to run to him. Hell, anyone's instincts would have been to run to him. Running to him would have entailed racing along the metal catwalk, which curved around the inside of the circular dome and hugged the gently sloping wall.

But I forced myself to stop. To think. To wait. Hard as it was. As nearly impossible as it was. I would be of no use to the boy if I died.

Although I couldn't sense him, I knew the vampire was here. He had to be here. The only beacon of light energy that I could see formed around the boy. The vampire, like other immortals I had seen, was immune to my detection.

But he was here. Somewhere. Watching me.

The hair on the back of my neck stood on end, and that was a completely human response to the feeling of being watched. I listened for breathing—other breathing—but heard nothing.

Wait, a flutter from above.

I looked up sharply. The tiny silhouette of a bat crossing in front of the window in the upper dome.

I remembered his words: *I'm here with the other bats.*

I turned right onto the catwalk, although I could have just as easily gone left, since the boy was directly opposite me. As I walked, I held onto the rusted guardrail, all too aware that the mesh flooring beneath me felt unsafe at best.

My footfalls echoed metallically. The whole damn catwalk seemed to sway. I scanned above and around, searching for a winged creature or the tall man with the bow tie.

I considered the possibility that I was dealing with a very powerful vampire. How long had this vampire been alive? Hundreds of years? Thousands? In that time period, what dark secrets had he uncovered? Invisibility, perhaps?

I had no clue, but I hoped like hell I didn't bump into him unexpectedly. That would just suck.

Something scuttled from above, too heavy for a bat. I snapped my head up.

Nothing there, other than beams and rafters and larger, seemingly random planks of wood. No vampire bat. Although the hiding spots were few and far between, he'd certainly had enough time to pick a good one.

He was watching me now. From somewhere. Of that, I had no doubt.

I was halfway to the boy, who was now trying to sit up. He couldn't see me in the dark, but he could certainly hear me coming. Hell, the dead could hear me coming, with all this rattling.

"It's going to be okay, Eddy," I said, although I was still thirty feet away. "I'll get you home soon."

"Oh, it's most assuredly *not* going to be okay," said a voice with a French accent above.

I looked up again, and this time, crawling down through the hole in the dome like a four-legged insect, was a man.

44.

As I watched him crawl through the hole, briefly blotting out the night sky, an uncontrollable shiver raced through me. He looked so inhuman, so unnatural, so alien.

I picked up my pace, moving rapidly now along the narrow catwalk, my weight causing the whole damn thing to shudder.

"Mommy?" cried the little boy.

"It's okay, baby," I said, moving faster still. The old catwalk wasn't designed for running. I could see the screws in the walls giving way, dust sifting down everywhere.

Sweet Jesus.

The man scuttled down along the inside of the dome, defying gravity, defying logic, defying sanity. I actually paused, watching him moving rapidly over beams and I-beams, around planks and fasteners, down the smooth inside paneling with no obvious handholds.

And all of this he did upside down. He should have fallen a hundred times over.

The angle he took was a good one, because now it put him directly between me and the boy. Within moments, the man in the bow tie flipped down and dropped smoothly to his feet. He turned to face me, straightening his dinner jacket and adjusting his bow tie.

"A pleasure to finally meet you, Samantha Moon," he said, his voice so heavily accented that he was difficult to understand. "I believe you have something I want."

The little boy had found his way to his knees, where he now sat on the mesh flooring. He turned his head this way and that, trying to see us, which I doubted he could. The interior of the dome was pitch black.

I had no intention of leaving here without the boy—and without my medallion. Yes, I wanted my cake and I wanted to eat it, too. I realized I needed more time. I needed to know what I was up against.

"What's your name?" I asked.

"Now," he said in his heavy French accent, "is that really important?"

Behind the gaunt figure, I saw for the first time the outline of a narrow door, maybe just a few feet from the little boy. Where the door led off to, I hadn't a clue. For all I knew it was a storage closet.

I said, "Then I guess you wouldn't mind if I call you Shithead."

He cocked his head slightly and his lips might have formed a smile. He was taller than me by a lot. Tall and thin and ghastly, the quintessential vampire. He advanced toward me, which was a good thing, I realized. Anything to get him away from the boy.

I held my ground.

The far less selfish thing for me to do was hand over the medallion and save the sick boy. But what about my son? How could I at least not first pursue another alternative?

Yes, I wanted my cake and to eat it, too.

It was then that I felt a heavy presence surround me, a sticky, sickly, foreign presence. It pushed on me, prodding me, trying to gain entrance. And just as suddenly the presence retreated.

"You are a strong one, *mademoiselle*," he said, frowning, clearly not happy. "Stronger than most. Too strong for even me to gain access."

"Lucky me," I said.

Whether or not the vampire could feel the ghost behind me, I didn't know, but I sure as hell could. Leland was clearly agitated, watching all of this from the shadows of the door, and I had an idea, recalling how the teen ghost had nearly manifested a physical hand for me to grab.

Leland, sweetie, I thought. *I need your help.*

Although behind me, I saw in my mind's eye

the young man suddenly perk up, his countenance brightening. He didn't speak, but I had his attention.

When one is open to such communication, words and thoughts tend to be the same, and so I focused my thoughts on the door behind the boy.

Where does this lead to, Leland?

An image was returned to me, one of a long and narrow hallway, similar to the one that had granted us access to within the dome. Leland had recognized the door.

Good, I thought. *Thank you.*

As quickly as I could, I explained what I needed. He nodded eagerly and disappeared. To where he went, I hadn't a clue. Would he help me? I didn't know that, either. I was noticing that ghosts, although quite social, weren't the best communicators.

I turned my attention back to the tall man who was watching me curiously. "I have lived a long, long time, Miss Moon," he said. "I'm tired of these old bones. I'm tired of this world, of this race. I'm tired of feeding...constantly feeding. Mostly I'm tired of the loneliness. The eternal loneliness. You will feel it someday, Miss Moon, if you haven't already."

His words were oddly hypnotic, captivating me in ways that I hadn't experienced before. I suspected this creature before me had mastered various levels of hypnotism or persuasion, or whatever the hell he was doing with his haunting voice.

I shook my head, cleared my thoughts, and imagined a sort of psychic barrier between me and this son-of-a-bitch. Except I didn't need a barrier. I needed ear plugs.

"I choose a French accent because I have lived most often in Paris, and this accent suits me. I enjoy hearing it. But I could just as easily switch to Baroque or German or ancient languages of which you would have no comprehension. This will be you someday, Miss Moon. When all those you love are long gone, when you find yourself alone yet again, speaking dead languages, and seeking new lands, new faces, new loves, new hunting grounds. And when even these places have been used up, you will set out again. And again. Forever seeking. But never finding."

"Are you quite done, Shithead?"

He paused and smiled. "You are a rare treat. I do not want to kill you, but I will. Please give me the medallion, then take the boy and be gone."

"Maybe," I said.

He cocked his head, and was about to speak when we both heard it. The squeak of a door being opened, perhaps for the first time in decades.

Bow Tie looked back just in time to see a brightly energetic being appear in the doorway.

Leland, and he had fully manifested. He was reaching for Eddy, having solidified enough to take the boy's hand.

Bow Tie growled furiously and lunged backwards.

I didn't growl, but I lunged, too.

45.

I had a small advantage since I was already facing forward.

I quickly covered the ground between us, and before Bow Tie could pick up any real speed, I hurled myself onto his back.

I had a brief glimpse of Leland, now fully manifested, gripping Eddy's hand, before the vampire and I toppled over the railing and fell briefly through space...

Unfortunately, the gangly bastard landed on me. I slammed my head hard, stars bursting behind my eyelids. The pain was severe but only fleeting. Already, my head was clearing, and as I looked up, past the vampire on top of me, I could see the ghost teen slipping back through the side door, gently pulling the little boy with him.

With any luck, the boy would never know that an honest-to-God ghost was leading him through the dark hallway.

Bow Tie looked wildly up, too, just as Leland and the boy spirited away through the narrow door. He made a move to get up, but I moved, too. I bucked my legs hard and sent the asshole flying over me, where he crashed hard, knocking over all sorts of shit that I couldn't see from my present position.

I stood and turned.

"Leave him alone," I said. "It's between you and me now."

The vampire, who had briefly disappeared behind some toppled night tables and desks, now stood, easily rising to his feet. His arm, I saw, was badly dislocated at the elbow. He winced slightly as he held it out, and what he did next didn't surprise me, although it caused the bile to rise up in the back of my mouth.

He gripped his forearm below the elbow and twisted and wrenched until his arm was back in place. All of this was accompanied by horrific sounds of bone grating against bone, of tendons grinding. He briefly made a face, but was soon opening and closing his hand. He next flexed his arm and seemed pleased with the results.

He looked at me.

"You are strong, little one. Stronger than most. You are a very unusual creature. Who made you?"

"Made me?"

"Who ended your mortal life, dear? And gave you immortality?"

"Let's not worry about that."

He stepped over the desk in one big stride, his long legs making the move seemingly effortless. As he did so, something else fell and settled behind him, kicking up even more dust, all of which plumed around like a personal thunderstorm. He stepped out of the dust and faced me.

"Yes, Kingsley said you would be a feisty one, but he never told me just how powerful you were."

My jaw dropped. "Kingsley?"

"Oh? You didn't realize that he's a good friend of mine? Or, rather, a client of mine." He cocked his head, clearly enjoying the obvious shock on my face. "Why, who do you think told me about the medallion, my dear?"

Now my jaw dropped open, and I felt as if someone had sucker punched me. Bow Tie began circling me, not approaching me directly, but in a circuitous route, as if sizing me up. There wasn't much to size up, trust me.

"And who do you think supplies him with his blood for his many...guests."

"Many guests?"

"Oh, I assume he has many guests. After all, I keep the red stuff coming fairly regularly."

I thought of the blood I had drank just a few weeks ago. It had come from *him*. This bastard. And where had Bow Tie gotten it? No doubt a most unwilling donor.

I felt sick. I felt betrayed. I felt pissed.

"Oh, don't be too hard on the big oaf," said Bow Tie. "I can be very persuasive when I want to be. You see, not everyone can resist me as you did. Not even Kingsley. Unfortunately for him, and you, he let it slip that something of great importance had turned up. And all it took were a few suggestions, a few tonal changes in my voice, and soon he was telling me everything I needed to know. I doubted the big bad wolf had any clue just how desperately I've been looking for your medallion. I knew it was in the area, and I had even narrowed down the city. Clues, rumors, whispers. All of which I paid attention to."

Some of my anger toward Kingsley had abated. But still. Why had Kingsley even mentioned the medallion, or even hinted at it? Big oaf indeed. And how could Kingsley befriend such a fucking piece of shit like Bow Tie?

And what most pissed me off was this: who was Kingsley sharing the blood with, if not me? At last count, I had only had two glasses of the "red stuff."

Big picture, Sam, I thought. *Deal with Kingsley later.*

As we circled, I reached down and felt for the medallion...only to discover my jeans had torn during the fall from the catwalk.

Oh, shit!

Panic ripped through me until I felt the familiar bulge of the disc. Not risking my torn pocket, I extracted the medallion, and as I did so, Bow Tie nearly dove at me. But he kept his composure. Instead, a strange light flared in his eyes. I certainly had his entire attention. The exhaustion I had seen earlier was gone, replaced now with desperation.

I did the only thing I could think of to keep the medallion safe.

I slipped the leather strap over my head, dropping the medallion down inside my blouse— and that's when it happened.

Boy, did it happen.

46.

"No!" shouted the vampire, his voice echoing everywhere.

To my utter shock, the medallion began burning my chest, so much so that I yelped. Steam was coming off my flesh, rising up from my blouse.

"You stupid girl!" he spat angrily. "You stupid, stupid girl. Do you realize what you've done?"

I looked up, confused as hell and wincing. The burning was not pleasant.

Bow Tie stepped closer. "You've sealed the medallion to yourself forever."

"I don't understand—"

"Of course not, because you're a stupid girl."

Pain or not, the guy was pissing me off. "Say that again, asshole, and see what happens."

But he was right. I reached down and immediately winced. My skin was tender, but already it was healing, and forming *over* the medallion. Amazingly, horrifyingly, the golden disk was now embedded *into* my chest.

Oh, no. No, no, no!

Bow Tie was shaking his head. "You and the medallion are one, forever, *mademoiselle*. Perhaps good for you, but not for me. And certainly not for your little one, whom you had hoped to save from an eternity of...this. There's no way to remove it." He paused and cocked his head. "Well, there is *one* way."

He pulled out a small pistol from inside his coat pocket. He pointed it at me haphazardly. "It's true. I cannot die from silver. Not anymore. Not ever." He leveled the weapon at me. "But you are not so fortunate, my dear. Five silver bullets. Only one needs to find your heart."

Not everyone is a great shot, even vampire assholes. The agency teaches you to be a moving target, which is always harder to hit than a stationary one.

I dove right, rolling just as the first shot was fired. The sound was so damn loud and echoing that it appeared he fired dozens of time.

I rolled again and had a brief glimpse of the vampire calmly taking aim. It's a surreal experience having someone take aim at you with a gun. To want to hurt you, to kill you.

All the talk of immortality was out the window.

With a simple silver bullet, my six-year immortal run would be over.

They say your life flashes before your eyes, but mine didn't. Not then. I only thought of Tammy and Anthony. That's it. No more. I didn't think of Fang or my sister or even Kingsley. I thought only of my children and what would happen to them without their freaky mother.

I rolled again when he fired. This time I felt an impact in my right shoulder. I cried out, clutching my shoulder, incapable of rolling or even really moving.

"Hurts, doesn't it?" said the vampire. "We are elemental creatures, finely attuned to the days and nights. We crave the metals in blood: zinc, iron, copper, magnesium. Is it no surprise, then, that another metal, silver, can destroy us? Well, some of us."

He seemed to smile, but it was hard to tell. Tears had burst from my eyes. The pain was intense. Too intense. I could barely focus or function.

He leveled the gun again, and I could not imagine more pain. I could not imagine another impact. I couldn't handle it. It would be too much. Way too much.

I turned away, my reflexes still amazingly sharp.

The bullet went through my neck. The shock sent me into a spasm. I went from clutching my shoulder to clutching my neck. The bullet had exited the side of my neck, exploding out, leaving a massive crater behind. Blood pumped over my hands, down over my shirt, down into my windpipe and lungs. I choked and gagged and flopped on the ground, drowning in my own blood.

Except I didn't need air to breathe, and so I wasn't really drowning.

I backed away, clutching my throat, blood gushing everywhere. The wounds were capable of closing. I tried to cough but couldn't. I felt like I was drowning, but I wasn't.

Bow Tie stepped closer and took careful aim.

Somewhere inside me, I had kept count of the bullets. Three shots. Two left. So far I was alive. So far he had missed my heart.

He stepped closer and took dead aim.

"Missed again," he said. "But not this time. I hope to see you in the next life."

I tried to move, but I slipped on my own blood, I fell to my back, still clutching my bleeding throat. All thoughts of my kids were gone. I only saw darkness. I only saw the bastard standing over me, taking careful aim at my chest.

And that's when I saw something else. Something else moving rapidly, leaping down from the catwalk above and covering the space between us in a blink of an eye. Something impossibly big, impossibly powerful.

Impossibly, it was Kingsley.

47.

A shot was fired, but it went wild.

It went wild because the great dark creature who had bounded over the railing and landed on the floor twenty feet below had slammed hard into the vampire. The force of the collision was enough to send the tall vampire hurtling off to one side, crashing beyond my field of blurred vision.

The gunshot had surely been as loud and echoing as the others had been, but to me it sounded distant and faint. I was seriously losing it and losing it fast.

I had a ground's-eye view of what happened next, although the images were sometimes too fast for even me to fully grasp.

The dark shadow was indeed Kingsley. He was

in human form, which was no surprise since this was not a night of a full moon. But there was something about him. Something that was hard for my fading mind to grasp. But he seemed bigger, impossibly fast, and so damn...inhuman.

I tried to sit up, but I couldn't. Instead, I rolled my head toward the action, and as I did so, I felt the gristle and bone in my neck crunch. More blood pumped free and I choked all over again. And as I choked, a presence hovered over me. A handsome, smiling, angelic face. A face with a bloody lower jaw.

Leland was here and he was kneeling next to me, trying his best to hold my head in his transparent arms that faded in and out of solidity.

From this position, I watched with horrific fascination as a battle waged. The vampire was fast. Perhaps too fast for Kingsley. But every now and then the big guy would catch the fast-moving blood sucker with a powerful blow. To my horror, I saw that Kingsley's face was bloodied already. The faster-moving vampire had already landed blow after blow.

Leland crouched next to me, still clutching my bleeding face, watching the scene as well. I briefly wondered where Eddy was but knew he had to be safe somewhere.

Kingsley hadn't transformed, but he had taken on the mannerisms of a cornered wolf. He often crouched, his back hunched. Deep-throated growls reverberated continuously, some louder than others, all ferocious-sounding.

As the action moved across the floor of the dome, I turned my head to follow it, or tried to. Mostly I moved my eyes, all too aware that a deep darkness was encroaching from my peripheral vision. Two silver bullets had hit me. One of them, I was certain, was still lodged in my shoulder. The other, I was equally certain, had gone straight through my neck, exploding out its side.

That's going to leave a mark.

Vampire and werewolf were a blur. Fists flying. Blood flying. Shredded clothing flying. At one point, Kingsley grabbed hold of the Frenchman, and pummeled him mercilessly with fists that looked, from my perspective, as big as anvils. Bone crunched against bone.

One moment Kingsley was pummeling the son-of-a-bitch, and the next the French bastard was gone, having squirmed his way free, moving quickly.

Now the two men faced off. Kingsley, I saw, was badly beaten up, his clothing completely shredded. For all of Kingsley's might, he couldn't keep up with the speed of the Frenchman.

"Until we meet again," said the Frenchman, and in a blink, his clothing, including that damn bow tie, burst from his body. Before us was a massive winged creature. Next to me, Leland squeaked loud enough to be heard in the physical world and huddled next to me, afraid even in death. Kingsley stood unmovingly before the winged creature, taking great, heaving breaths.

A moment later, the creature's monstrous wings flapped once, twice, and then he was airborne. A few flaps later and he had burst through the top of the dome, raining wood and brick around us. Kingsley immediately shielded me, protecting me with his thick body. As he did so, blood from his wounded face dripped over me.

He looked down at me with wide, amber eyes. "I'm so sorry, Samantha. I'm so very sorry."

And that's when I blacked out.

48.

I saw the yellow light first.

Two glowing disks that hovered in front of me. One of the lights was picking at me, digging into my shoulder, causing me excruciating pain. It was the pain that had forced me back to consciousness.

I opened my eyes slowly and saw two faces hanging over me. One of them belonged to Detective Hanner, my female vampire friend, and the other was an unknown man. The unknown man was finishing up working on my shoulder. He picked up a metal dish and held it up, rattling it. Hanner peered inside. "Good work, doc."

He said, "I would normally be stitching her up but, as you can see, her wound is already healing."

"Again, thank you, doctor. Speak to no one as

you leave."

"Of course." He nodded, grabbed a small handbag, and left through the back door of an ambulance.

"This is beginning to be a habit," said Hanner. She was, of course, referring to one of our previous meetings when she and I had ended up in an ambulance outside of an Indian casino in Simi Valley. "And don't try to speak, Sam. Doctor Hector tells me that your throat is shredded to hell. Even for us that will take a few hours to heal. Oh, and don't worry. He's on our payroll, so to speak. So your secret is safe with him."

Full comprehension of where I was or what was going on hadn't fully settled in. I heard voices everywhere. Shouting. One woman crying. A man crying, too. Sirens.

"You see, there are a few carefully selected mortals out there who work with us. The good doctor is one such man."

Why he would help, I had no idea, but I couldn't think about that now. She saw my eyes shift towards the sound of nearby crying.

"Yes, we're still at the Mission Inn. The boy you saved is with his parents, and we can only thank you. You are proving to be quite the superhero, Samantha." She leaned over and inspected my throat. "Nasty business, made worse because it was a silver bullet. But it will heal soon enough."

I heard more sirens, some nearby, and she saw

the alarm in my eyes. "Not to worry, Sam. We're already forgotten by the Riverside Police. I have a few talents of my own, and one of them is, let's just say, *persuasion*. As far as the police are concerned, we're just another ambulance waiting to help."

I soon recognized another voice from outside, coming closer.

Hanner reached over and patted my knee. "I imagine you're going to want to speak with Kingsley." She smiled warmly and touched the back of my hand. "Well, you know what I mean."

As she left, Kingsley Fulcrum and his massive bulk eased into the ambulance.

49.

"Doctor Hector tells me you can't speak, maybe that's just as well," said Kingsley. He had eased down at the foot of the gurney. I think my end of the metal bed had risen an inch or two.

Kingsley was hunched into a sort of cannonball, his meaty knees up around his chest. He looked uncomfortable and didn't seem to know what to do with his thick arms. He was dressed in another shirt, clearly one that wasn't his own, since that had been bloodied and shredded. His own wounds had long since healed.

He reached out and touched my right ankle which was poking out of the thick blanket covering me. I flinched and withdrew it. He nodded to himself. "I deserved that. I deserve, in fact, for you to never talk to me again. I should consider myself lucky that I have you here, alone, in this small place, so that you are more or less forced to hear my apology."

I was still in some pain, as the effects of the silver bullet still lingered. Perhaps there were trace elements of silver still lodged in my muscle tissue? Lord, I hoped not. Or, more than likely, my actual muscles and tendons and flesh supernaturally mending themselves.

Lord, I'm such a freak.

Kingsley's longish hair spilled over his collar. Known as a maverick lawyer, Mr. Fulcrum propagated the image by keeping his hair long and thick and lustrous. Then again, maybe his flowing locks were a result of his own particular wolfish condition. Now, for the first time in a long time, Kingsley looked at me so tenderly that my heart heaved.

"You took a helluva beating tonight, kid. I'm sorry you had to go through that alone. I should have been there earlier to help." He made a move to pat my ankle again, but stopped himself. This time I wasn't so sure I would have moved my leg. "You deserved better. You deserved a friend who supported you through thick and thin, good and bad. Who am I to tell you how to run your life, how to deal with your dying boy? Who am I to play God from afar? You made the best choice you could, and I should have been there to support you. My God, I'm an ass, and I almost lost you forever because of it. Look at you, babe. You can't even talk. Your poor throat. And you did this all to help another boy, risking life and limb and the very medallion you need to help your son, and I couldn't even be there for you."

Now I did something that surprised even me. I leaned forward and took his warm hand. It took both of mine to comfortably hold one of his, and we gripped each other like this for a few minutes.

I wanted to tell him that he did come, that he did help me, that he did save my ass, but I couldn't speak, nor could I penetrate Kingsley's thoughts. An immortal, he was closed to me.

He chuckled lightly, running his thick thumb over the back of my hand. "I bet you're wondering how I came to be there on time. Well, the *on time* part was dumb luck. The being here part, not so much. I realized I had made an egregious error when I had mentioned the medallion to Dominique." He caught my raised eyebrows. "Oh, you didn't know his name?"

Ah, so the bastard had a name. Dominique. I was certain I hadn't seen the last of him.

Kingsley continued, "I can't be certain, but I think Dominique has been around long enough to read the minds of fellow immortals. But that's no excuse. I've been around long enough to learn how to guard myself from such an attack. I suspected he scanned my thoughts and knew that you and that damn medallion were heavy on my thoughts. He then mentioned something about it and I felt oddly...*compelled* to tell him what I knew. He's a bastard. A sneaky bastard, but what do you expect from a blood dealer? Still, I should have been more guarded in his presence."

Kingsley looked away and I wanted to desperately ask him about the blood. Who else was he sharing it with? Another woman? Should I even care if it was another woman? Kingsley had been famous as a womanizer. Did his harem of women also include vampires? It seemed so unlikely. But my thoughts were cut short when Kingsley went on.

"I knew he was staying at the Mission Inn. In fact, he's been here for quite some time. After I blurted out the info on the medallion, I was on edge, nervous. I should have warned you. Instead, I lashed out at you, perhaps more angry at myself for not keeping your potentially dangerous artifact a secret. And when I heard about the kidnapping at the hospital, it seemed fairly obvious to me what had happened, and I headed out to the Mission Inn immediately. I have fairly good instincts, too, and, as you might imagine, a helluva sniffer."

I laughed lightly, which tore at my throat. I reached for it immediately, wincing.

"Easy," he said. "No more laughing, young lady. Anyway, I'm quite familiar with your scent and I was soon on the trail."

What every woman wants to hear, I thought.

I think he read my expression. "Oh, nothing bad, of course. Your scent is all your own, and the way my own supernatural hard-wiring works, I can distinguish individual scents from thousands, even millions, of other scents. Call it my gift. Hey, you turn into a giant vampire bat and I can smell feet."

I slapped his hand and stifled my laughter. He squeezed my hand tenderly and looked at me so deeply that I felt a stirring deep in my heart. Love?

Damn him.

"Anyway, I was soon following a winding pair of stairs when I came across a rather strange young man. Poor guy looked like he'd been through hell, face bloodied and all. He immediately led the way down a side hallway, up another flights of stairs, and that's when I heard the gunshots. I came running, fast. Where the young man went off to, or who he was, I haven't a clue—"

Leland had, of course, been there by my side, comforting me the best way he knew how. A sweet guardian angel with a crush.

Kingsley went on, "And before I knew it, I was on top of Dominique and I think you know the rest. The boy, Eddy, I believe, is safely with his family and apparently unhurt. Interestingly, he too spoke of a young man leading him out to safety. I suspect it was the same young man who had helped me. Do you know him, Sam?"

I simply nodded.

"Well, he's an unsung hero and there are a lot of people who want to thank him. The police are looking, of course, for the man who kidnapped Eddy, but for the most part, the police are unaware of your involvement, Sam. Thanks in part to

Detective Hanner. She can put quite a spell on people. She even went back and cleaned up your blood. Mine, too."

He continued stroking my hand, and as he did so, I saw the tears forming in his eyes. The moment his tears formed, my own came running free, too.

Damn him.

"I don't expect you to forgive me, Sam, for being a holier-than-thou ass, but if you can find it in your heart to give me one more chance, I promise I will do my best to never hurt you again. You see..." And now he covered my two hands with both of his, and never have I felt so protected. "I think I'm falling for you, Sam, and I don't want to screw it up any worse than I already have."

His words caught me by surprise. Mostly, because they echoed my own thoughts.

"Take care of yourself, kiddo, and take care of your little one, too. You're a good mother, and I respect you more than you can possibly know."

He leaned over the gurney and kissed me lightly on my lips, then turned away and headed out, pushing through the ambulance's door.

50.

I awoke by my son's side in the early afternoon.

With Dominique still out there, it was hard to truly feel at peace, although I suspected any attack now would be on me personally, and not my son, since the medallion was still sealed to my chest.

Where Dominique had gone, I hadn't a clue. But I would be ever vigilant for him and perhaps others like him, especially since he had proven to be such a bastard.

I soon got the news I was dying for. The doctors were releasing Anthony later today. For now, two policemen had guard duty just outside his door. The hospital, apparently, was taking all necessary security precautions, especially since little Eddy's abductor had not been found.

I absently felt for the medallion that had melded into my flesh. I hated the irony. I possessed the very artifact that would have returned Anthony's mortality, an artifact that, apparently, was sealed to me forever.

Or so said the vampire, Dominique. I wanted a second opinion. In the least, I still wanted to find Archibald Maximus, whoever the hell he was.

My cell rang. I glanced at the faceplate. Restricted call. It was Detective Sherbet. I was sure of it.

I clicked on briefly and told him to call me back in five minutes since I was at the hospital. He called me back in four, just as I was exiting through the sliding glass doors.

"You did good, kid," he said.

"Thank you," I whispered. I still had not gotten the full use of my voice back. Not to mention that my shoulder still hurt.

"Interestingly, no one mentioned you in any reports. Only a young man who saved the day."

"God bless him."

"Apparently the little boy had been held captive, albeit briefly, within one of the domes. They found damage to the ceiling and what appeared to be an epic fight. You wouldn't happen to know anything about this, would you, Sam?"

"Do you really want to know?"

"I want to know everything, dammit."

"I've told you more than I should have."

"That's not good enough. Not in this case."

"Soon, Detective. I've had a rough night."

"I bet. You vampires are weird. Take care of yourself, Samantha, and expect a visit from me soon."

"Looking forward to it."

"Don't sass me," he said, chuckling, and hung up.

I was about to head inside when I got another call. This one was a local Orange County number. It was probably work related but I wasn't interested. I was about to hang up when I got an overwhelming sense that I should definitely pick up.

Damn psychic ability.

I clicked on, immediately regretting it because my sunscreen wasn't applied as thick as it should have been. Already I was feeling the first wave of some serious pain.

"Samantha Moon?" asked a pleasant young man.

"You got her," I said.

"You removed a book from our library the other day and we would like it returned."

"Who is this?"

"I'm with the university."

I frowned. "How did you know about the book? How did you know it was me?"

But he ignored my question and asked cheerily: "We would like our book back, Miss Moon."

I forgot about the heat, about the searing pain. "I don't have it anymore."

"I see," said the voice, somehow even more

cheerily. "Then there will be a fine. We will need that taken care of immediately."

"A fine? How much?"

"I think you know the price, Miss Moon." And the moment he said that, the medallion in my chest pulsed with heat of its own. "I will be expecting you soon."

And he hung up.

51.

I was back at the university library, and this time I was certain a bastard in a bow tie wasn't following me.

Anthony wouldn't be released for another few hours and Tammy was with Mary Lou. Feeling an odd sense that I was either stepping into a trap, or into something extraordinary, I moved through the busy ground floor, and on an impulse I stopped at the main desk.

"Who works in the Occult Reading Room?" I asked the flirty young clerk.

"In the Occult Reading Room? No one. It's a self-service reading room. But I could help you if you—"

"Thank you," I said, and turned away. I headed

over to the bank of elevators. In a daze, admittedly.

At the third floor, which was as empty as the first time I had been here, with my curiosity and wariness growing exponentially, I made my way down an empty aisle, stepping lightly over the dull acrylic flooring. With each step, my shoulder ached. My throat was still raw and red and for now I kept a scarf around it. The air conditioner hummed from seemingly everywhere.

At the end of the aisle I came to the far wall. Ahead of me was the opening to the Occult Reading Room. Would the same young man be there? The young man with the bright eyes and the slightly pointed beard, a young man I hadn't thought much about the first time I had seen him, but who was now very much the object of my attention.

Prepared for just about anything, I moved forward, all too aware that the medallion on my chest was growing warmer and warmer.

***

The same young man was there, and he was once again sitting behind what I had assumed was an employee desk, but was, in fact, just an oversized reading desk.

I sat cautiously opposite him, noting that my own inner alarm system was as quiet as could be. In fact, I even felt oddly at peace, perhaps for the first time in a long, long time.

"You don't really work here," I said, as I sat my

purse on the floor next to me.

"Not officially," he said, dipping his head slightly, apologetically.

He couldn't have been more than twenty-five, perhaps even as young as twenty. He looked like a student, surely. Other than the bright twinkle in his eye and his pointy beard, he looked unremarkable.

"Who are you?" I asked.

"Archibald Maximus, of course," he said. "You can just call me Max, though."

I stared at him a long time. His aura was violet. A beautiful violet unlike anything I had ever seen. "How old are you, Max?"

He gave me a half smile. "Does it matter?"

"I guess not," I said. I liked the way Max looked at me. He didn't stare rudely. In fact, he seemed to find great pleasure in looking at me, as if he were soaking me up, remembering my every detail. Normally, I don't like to draw attention to myself and I like to be ignored. But sometimes I make exceptions. "You're not a student here, are you?"

He smiled warmly. "No."

"And you're not twenty-something, either?"

"Let's just say no."

We looked at each other some more. I noticed now how perfectly groomed his beard was. I also noticed that his blue eyes were not really blue...holy hell, were they violet?

"I...I don't have your book," I said.

"I know."

"I don't know what happened to it."

"That's okay."

"Do I still owe a fine?"

His lips broke into a wide smile, his cheeks rising high enough that the fine point of his beard wasn't so fine.

"I don't think the library would appreciate me taking fines for books that don't officially exist."

"I don't understand."

"It's okay if you don't understand. There's lots I don't understand, too. That's half the fun: finding answers." He leaned forward a little and his gaze locked onto the area just beneath my throat, an area that was now throbbing with real warmth.

"Ah, I see you're wearing the medallion. Or, more accurately, it's wearing you."

Which should have been a highly unlikely statement, since the medallion was currently concealed beneath my shirt.

"I...was protecting it. I had no idea it would..."

"Attach itself to you?"

"Yes."

"Would you like for me to remove it?"

"Yes. But I had heard—"

"The seal was permanent?"

"Yes."

"Normally, yes. But I'm fairly familiar with it. Would you mind?" he asked.

I shook my head and he got up from behind the desk and stepped around to me.

"Just try to relax," he said.

He put his hands on my shoulders, which sent a

shiver of warm energy through me, charging me from the inside. Next he moved his fingers around my throat and slipped them down inside my shirt.

I gasped and felt a different kind of thrill.

His searching hands found the medallion, where he rested the flat of his palms over it. There was no pain, just a sense of...release.

A moment later he removed his hands, and held up the gleaming medallion. He grinned.

I was relieved beyond words. There was hope again. There was hope my son could live a normal life.

"Now, Sam, what would you like to do with this?"

But I was having difficulty speaking. I was so afraid to have hope, so afraid to believe. I tried speaking again: "I had heard that the medallion..." but I couldn't get the words out.

"You had heard that it could reverse vampirism?"

"Yes," I said, but I was terrified to hear his answer. Oh, sweet Jesus. What if he couldn't do it? Or what if he said no? What would I do then?

"Yes," he said, smiling. "The medallion can do this. Or, rather, the magic encoded within it can."

"And you...you can decode this?"

He nodded. "I can, Sam. And before you ask, yes, I will help your little one."

Relief flooded me. So much so that I couldn't stop shaking. He reached out and took my hand.

"You've had a rough few days, haven't you?"

I could only nod as the shaking, the relief, overcame me.

"You're never alone, Sam. Ever. As hard as life might seem, there's always hope. There's always a way, and there's always love. Always."

I waited before I was certain I could speak, then asked, "How did you know I was looking for you?"

"How do you know *I* wasn't looking for *you*?" he asked, eyes twinkling. He saw my confusion and smiled sweetly. "Very few call my name, Sam, but when they do, I listen."

I couldn't speak. I could only nod my thanks.

He said, "Now give me a few minutes. Feel free to peruse the books, but stay away from the ones that call out to you. They're trouble."

I told him I would be careful, and he slipped away into a side room and closed the door. A few minutes later, he returned holding a small glass container with a cork cap, filled with amber liquid.

"Have your son drink this tonight. He will sleep soundly for twenty-four hours, and will awaken with little memory of the past few days."

"And he will be...human?"

"As human as ever."

"And the medallion?" I asked.

He motioned to the amber liquid. "The medallion is no more."

I raised the glass container, mystified. "It's in here?"

He winked. "Distilled through, let's just say, highly-advanced alchemical means. And

Samantha?"

"Yes?"

"There's only enough for one."

"Somehow I knew that."

"Remember, Samantha, there's always an answer. Somewhere. You just have to look."

I hugged the young man as hard as I could, and thanked him. When I finally pulled away, I saw that my own tears had stained his white shirt.

"I'm always here, Samantha, if you ever need anything."

"Here in the Occult Reading Room?"

He grinned and winked. "There's a lot to read. Oh, I have one question: How did you come upon my name?"

I told him about the creepy old gnome who lived in Fullerton. As I spoke, Max pulled on his pointed beard.

"And he bargained for your son's life?" he asked.

"I'm horrible, I know. I was desperate."

"Not to fear, Sam. One cannot bargain with another's life. Ever."

I looked at him sharply. "What do you mean?"

"I mean, your son is safe."

"And the creepy old gnome?"

"The creepy old gnome will never bother you again."

I hugged him for a second time. Somehow, even tighter.

52.

It was a week later.

Summer was in full bloom and I was working a few cases. I had two cheating spouse cases and an undercover assignment working for a shipping company to find the reason for their occasional missing shipments. Two nights ago, I had gone on a date with Kingsley, to the musical premier of *Annie* in Los Angeles. He had kissed me goodnight and bowed slightly, and I was reminded all over again of his grace and charm and just how old he really was. Yes, we still had our issues, but to his credit he had dropped his loser client once and for all.

Fang was there, too. Always texting, IMing and emailing. During one of our exchanges, I told him that Kingsley and I were going to explore a relationship together, but I always wanted Fang as my friend.

He had paused for a few minutes before answering. When he did, he said that, of course, we would always be friends and that he was happy for me. To his credit, he appeared to be happy for me, but I could feel his hurt. We were, after all, still deeply connected.

Danny had visited the kids once, and although he seemed pleased that his son was alive and well and not a freak, as he liked to call me, I could see that his old suspicion was back. The fear was back. The hate was back.

Admittedly, I almost preferred Danny like this. I could handle his hate and suspicion. His flirting this past week had just been damn creepy.

Now it was a Saturday evening and I would work the night shift later. It was dinner time, and I called the kids in from the backyard where they were playing on a Slip N' Slide. Both were as red as tomatoes from their sun block having long since worn off, and never had I been more happy to see a sunburn on my son. Anthony was showing no ill effects from either the vampirism or the Kawasaki Disease, either.

My son was back, alive and healthy. Had I altered his soul's journey? Maybe. Had I played with his karma? No doubt.

But he was back. Oh, yes, he was back.

Dripping and arguing, they came running inside, snatching hot dogs and chips. A few minutes later,

Mary Lou and her family arrived. My sister gave me a big hug and Anthony an even bigger hug.

We all settled in with hot dogs and chips—or water, in my case—and put in a movie. About halfway through the movie a strong and foul smell permeated my living room, and that's when the looks started.

"Mommy did it!" Anthony cried out, giggling.

"That's it," I said, grabbing him and throwing him over my legs, exposing his bony butt to the air. I was soon playing butt bongos off his little tush while he squealed with laughter. Soon Tammy joined in and so did my sister. There might have been some tickling thrown in for good measure.

It was later, at night, when I was putting Anthony to sleep when he looked up at me and said, "Thank you, Mommy."

"For what?"

"For what you did."

"What did I do?"

"You know, Mommy," he said, and reached up and hugged me tighter than he had ever hugged me before.

The End

About the Author:

J.R. Rain is an ex-private investigator who now writes full-time. He lives in a small house on a small island with his small dog, Sadie. Please visit him at www.jrrain.com.

Made in the USA
Monee, IL
03 June 2022

97421704R00125